Community Library of DeWitt & Jamesville
5110 Jamesville Road
DeWitt, NY 13078

The
LAND
of
ROAR

The
LAND
of
ROAR

JENNY
McLACHLAN
Illustrated by Ben Mantle

HARPER
An Imprint of HarperCollinsPublishers

Library of Congress Control Number: 2019955867

ISBN 978-0-06-298271-1

20 21 22 23 24   PC/LSCH   10 9 8 7 6 5 4 3 2 1

❖

First U.S. edition, 2020

Originally published in the UK in 2019 by Egmont UK

*For my girls, who never
stopped believing in Roar*

MITCH

ARCHIE PLAYGO

TANGLED F

ROAR
the END
st
the CROW's Nest
The BAD siDe
DUNGUN
by Rose
and ARTHUR

CHAPTER 1

There is a wizard in Grandad's attic.

I'm sitting in his garden looking up at the attic window, and I can clearly see a dark shape standing just behind the glass. I give my sister a nudge. "Look, Rose. You can see its pointy hat and everything!"

Rose swipes at the screen of her phone. "There isn't a wizard in the attic, Arthur. Leave me alone. I'm busy."

I glance over her shoulder and see that she's busy liking someone's picture of a puddle. When I look back at the window the strange shadow is still there. My eyes trace the outline of shoulders, a head, and a slightly crooked hat as I try to work out what it could be. . . . A reflection of the trees? Some rubbish Grandad's dumped up there?

Then I see something that makes goose bumps prickle my arms: a tiny white patch—like a puff of breath—is misting the glass. I squeeze my eyes shut and rub them. When I open them again the white patch has gone. I smile nervously. Mum's always saying I've got an overactive imagination.

"It's probably the inflatable skeleton," I say. "The one Grandad got for Halloween, and the hat could be from the dressing-up box—"

"Be quiet, Arthur," says Rose. "You're annoying me."

With a sigh I give up on Rose and wander around the garden. I peel some bark off a tree, kick a punctured football into a hedge, then hang from a branch. Tap, tap, tap goes Rose on her phone. I drop to the ground and look up at the attic window. "It's still there," I say.

"Arthur!" Rose snaps. "Will you shut up about wizards? I'm not going to play with you!"

I groan and flop back down on the grass. Every summer Mum and Dad leave us with Grandad while they go camping. It used to be brilliant. Rose and I would spend the whole week doing whatever we liked—building dens, swimming in the sea, eating cereal three times a day—but since Rose got her phone she's become totally boring.

"Om-pom-pom . . ." Grandad drifts out of his shed, his gray hair and beard standing out against his dark skin. He grins at me, then starts hacking at a bush with a pair of rusty hedge clippers.

"Grandad, have you put a dummy or something up in the attic?"

He laughs. "Not me, mate."

I turn back to Rose. She can't stare at her phone all day. "How about we check out the attic, then go and catch crabs off the end of the pier?"

"No."

"Play Ping-Pong?"

"No."

"Go to the arcade and pretend to be pirates and see if we can find money that's fallen out of the slot machines?"

She shakes her head in alarm. "No way!"

"But you used to love doing that."

"*You* used to love doing that, Arthur. I went along with it."

Suddenly Rose jumps to her feet and stuffs her phone into her pocket. Mazen Bailey, Grandad's next-door neighbor, has appeared on the trampoline in her garden. Mazen Bailey is a horrible person, but Rose worships her because she's thirteen, two years older than us, and has her own YouTube channel called *Totally Mazen!*

Rose scrambles onto the rubbish bin and leans over the wall. "Hi, Mazen!"

"*What* have you done to your hair?" shrieks Mazen, then she joins Rose at the wall and they begin a whispered conversation, every now and then glancing in my direction.

"Arthur," says Rose, "what was it you saw in the attic?"

I hesitate. They're smiling, waiting for me to say something stupid, so I say, "A shadow."

"Yeah, but what did the shadow *look like?*"

"A wizard," I mutter, making them burst out laughing. I feel my cheeks burn and I point at the window. "I'm not imagining it! Look!"

And they do look, but Rose shakes her head. "There's *nothing* there, Arthur!"

"There is. . . ." I protest, but then I realize she's right. The window is just a blank empty square. "You've got to stand in the right spot," I say, moving from side to side. "Make sure the sun isn't reflecting on the glass." But no matter what I do, I can't make the shape come back.

With a final giggle Mazen says she's got to go. "Come around later, Rose. You can try out my trampoline."

"Really?" cries Rose. "Thanks!"

Mazen disappears inside her house and Rose jumps off the rubbish bin.

"*Really?*" I say, imitating her gushy voice. "*Thanks!*"

Quick as a flash, Rose throws her arms around my legs and sends me crashing to the ground. Rose is good at rugby . . .

but I'm good at wriggling. I try to escape by twisting and turning like a snake, but Rose just tightens her viselike grip.

"Let go of me!" I shout.

"Not until you stop being annoying!"

"I'll stop being annoying"—I try and fail to kick her off—"when you stop being boring, which will be NEVER!"

Rose squeezes harder until my legs start to go numb. "*Drain*," she says in a deep, slow voice. "*DRAIN . . . DRAAAAIN . . .*"

This is something we used to do to each other—pretend we could drain each other of energy by holding on tight and not letting go. Rose hasn't done it for years, but it's still surprisingly effective. Already my legs feel weak and heavy, like lumps of concrete.

"Twins!" We look up and see Grandad standing over us. "I don't want to break up your game, but I thought you'd like to know there's a surprise waiting for you in the attic!"

We jump to our feet.

I *knew* I saw something up there. Grandad's surprises are legendary. He's built us a tree house, go-carts with working lights, and even a raft that we take on the river. Whatever he's done in the attic, I bet it involves that wizard!

"Race you!" I yell, making a dash for the back door.

I've only gone three paces when Rose overtakes me. She shoves me on my shoulder, shouting, "See you later, loser!"

I try to make my short legs work faster, but Rose is such a good runner and she drained me so well, there's no way

I can catch up with her. So instead I go with insulting her, and I shout the insult that I know annoys her the most, and I shout it all the way through the house and up the stairs.

"You look like me! You look like me! YOU LOOK LIKE ME!"

CHAPTER 2

"Whoa . . . ," I say, standing at the attic door.

I've not been up here for a few years, but it's even messier than I remember. Bags and boxes are piled knee-deep across the floor and toys are scattered everywhere. There are broken bikes and a canoe tucked into the eaves, and I can just see the old sofa buried under a pile of blankets. It's a dump, but just standing in this dusty, untidy room makes me happy. This is where Rose and I used to play—the best games that went on for hours.

"I can't see any surprise," says Rose, poking around behind the sofa.

My eyes go straight to the window. I'm expecting to see the inflatable skeleton, or a load of boxes . . . but there's nothing there at all. For a second I'm disappointed—I was so sure the wizard was going to be part of Grandad's surprise—but then the prickle of fear comes creeping back because *I'm sure* I saw something up here.

Just then Grandad comes wheezing into the room.

"So what do you think of your surprise?" he says.

I pull my eyes away from the window. "We can't find it."

Grandad laughs and throws his arms out wide. "That's because you're standing in it!"

Rose blinks. "What do you mean, Grandad?"

"*The attic* is your surprise. Isn't it amazing?"

Rose and I share a look of confusion. Grandad's done some pretty weird stuff over the years—including dyeing his beard green for Christmas—but he's never given us his attic as a present.

He looks at us eagerly. "Do you like it?"

I nod. "Yeah, it's really . . . surprising."

Rose is less polite. "Is this some sort of joke, Grandad?"

He walks around the messy room, kicking things out of his way. "I know it doesn't look like much at the moment, but once you've cleared it out, I'm going to turn it into a den for the two of you. I'll put a TV over there, replace the sofa, put a popcorn machine in the corner. Whatever you want. It will be yours!"

I smile as I imagine how amazing it will look. Even Rose's eyes light up, breaking her number-one rule of never showing she's into something. "I've *always* wanted a proper den," she says. "Not the sort of thing me and Arthur used to make with blankets. Can we have beanbags?"

Grandad laughs. "Shaped like burgers?"

And that's when my mind catches up with what

Grandad just said. "Hang on. What do you mean, once *you've* cleared it out?"

"Well, look around! How can I make you an amazing den if all this junk is up here?" He pushes a wobbly pile of boxes. "I'd like to help, but I can't, not with my asthma." To prove his point he bends over and breaks into a hacking cough.

"Inhaler," I say, and obediently he pulls out his asthma inhaler and has a puff.

"Nothing to worry about," he says, straightening up. "Now, after you've got the attic empty, we can spend the rest of the week painting."

Rose groans. "Do we have to, Grandad?"

I'm with Rose on this. In just over a week we start at Langton Academy—a huge secondary school that's packed full of big, scary kids and that has a no-talking-in-the-corridors rule—I do not want to spend my last days of freedom doing DIY.

"You have to if you want a den," says Grandad. Then he grabs a pile of comics and heads for the door. "I'll be in my shed."

For a moment Rose and I stand there staring at the chaos. Then Rose picks up a meter ruler—which for some reason is wrapped in tinfoil—and starts clearing a path through the middle of the junk. "This is my half," she says, then she tosses the ruler into the messier part of the attic, "and that's your half." Next she opens a cupboard and starts pulling out books. After a moment, she says, "No wizards in here, Arthur."

With a sigh I pick up a sports bag and start stuffing it full of *National Geographic* magazines.

Suddenly Rose gasps. "Hang on . . . I think I've found one!"

I can't resist looking up.

Rose is grinning and holding up a large dusty book. "My mistake. It's not a wizard. It's a French dictionary."

I go back to the magazines. Something tells me this is going to be a very long day.

CHAPTER 3

Rose decides that we're going to put everything in the garden before sorting out what's going to the dump and what's going to the thrift shop, and "Hurry up, Arthur!" soon becomes her favorite phrase. But it's hard to hurry up when there's so much cool stuff to look at.

I discover a magic set, a whole pillowcase stuffed full of Playmobil pirates, and I even find a wizard's hat perched on top of an oar. I wonder if this could be what I saw at the window, but the oar is right at the back of the attic. There's no way I could have seen it from the garden.

I put the hat on and creep up on Rose, planning to scare her, but when she turns around she just narrows her eyes and says, "Didn't you once have an imaginary friend who was a wizard?"

She's right, I did. His name was Wininja and he was stealthy and a bit magical.

"He was a wizard-*ninja*, Rose. Big difference."

She smiles. "Is he standing next to you right now, Arthur,

MiTch

ARChie PlAYGo

TANGLEDF

whispering in your ear?"

The moment she says this I have this sensation that someone *could be* standing next to me and I have to fight the urge to look. Rose goes back to her books and I glance around the attic, my eyes lingering on the darkest corners. "Hurry up, Arthur!" Rose snaps.

While Rose takes her bag downstairs, I decide to get started on the dressing-up box. I take out an armful of clothes and dump them on the floor. I'm just trying to detangle a ball of beards and wigs when I spot a candy tin buried at the bottom of the box.

I pull it out and feel the weight of it in my hands. It's round and dented, and has a picture of a soldier and a lady

ROAr the END → the CROW's Nest by ROSe and ARTHUR

on the front, and when I shake it I can hear something rattling around inside. I sit down and pry at the lid until it opens with a shower of rusty flakes. All that's inside is a foil chocolate wrapper and a large folded piece of paper. The piece of paper has the word *SECRIT!* written on the front in my own handwriting.

I stare at the thick, yellowing piece of paper, holding my breath as I wonder what I once thought was so secret. Carefully I unfold it and spread it out across the attic floor. It's a hand-drawn map, covered in tiny pictures and carefully written labels, something Rose and I must have made years ago.

The map is of a wobbly land almost cut in half by a

river. One side of this land is as colorful as a cartoon, with emerald-green trees and bright blue lakes. The other half has hardly any color at all. It's filled with blackened mountains, jagged gray cliffs, and forests of sticklike trees. Written along the top of the map, again in my spiky handwriting, is one word: ROAR.

"*Roar . . .*" The word sounds so familiar when I say it out loud.

My eyes follow the zigzag waves one of us had drawn across the sea, and suddenly I remember the way those waves crashed against the cliffs and how there were so many of them the sea seemed to churn and boil. Just when I'm thinking that this map must have been inspired by some place Mum and Dad took us on vacation, I remember something else: me and Rose bursting into this attic and shouting, "Let's play Roar!"

I smile. Roar isn't a real place. It's a game that Rose and I used to play, one that was so good, we drew a map of it.

As I gaze at the map, the game comes creeping back to me. I see mountain ranges stretched between the folds of the paper and a curving coastline dotted with coves and cliffs. There's a cluster of gumdrop-shaped islands labeled *Archie Playgo*, a castle rising out of the sea, and three dragons soaring through the sky. Butterflies, or maybe fairies, are dotted everywhere and sly-looking unicorns peer from between trees. I can't actually remember sitting next to Rose and drawing these things, but still my mind tingles with recognition and something else. Something I can't quite put my finger on.

Rose's footsteps pull me back to the attic.

"What's that?" she says, kneeling next to me.

"It's a map we drew of Roar."

She frowns. "What's Roar?"

"That game we used to play. You must remember!"

"Not really. . . . We played loads of games up here."

"But Roar was our favorite. There were wizards and mermaids and we'd fight and have adventures. We played it loads!"

Rose looks at me with wide, amused eyes. "If you say so, Arthur."

I point at the blackened castle rising out of the sea. It's labeled *The Crow's Nest*. "That's where the bad guy lived, and look"—I tap a black circle—"That's my ninja-wizard's cave. There he is!" A smiling face peeks out of the cave, a pointed hat sitting on his head. "I'm sure you had a friend too . . ."

Rose searches the gumdrop-shaped islands until she spots something: a girl's head poking out of the sea. She has blue hair drifting around her and the word *Mitch* written by the tip of her silver tail. "*Mitch* . . . ," says Rose, frowning. Then she smiles. "She was a mermaid-witch!"

"With a bad temper—"

"And webbed fingers and a magic tail!"

Sun streams through the window, and outside the birds sing. Just for a moment, it's like it was when we were little, when we used to finish each other's sentences and make stuff up faster than we could think it.

Together, we stare at the map. Suddenly Rose shakes her head and jumps to her feet. She grabs a bulging trash bag and drags it toward the door. "Hurry up, Arthur," she calls over her shoulder, "or we'll never get our den."

When I hear the bag thumping down the stairs I turn back to the map. I can't resist.

My eyes wander over pathways and streams and mountain passes, and I start to lose myself in this strange place we invented. Then something catches my eye—a flicker of movement, a flash of light—and I find myself staring at the Crow's Nest. I see something that I missed before. A face is looking out of a window. The face is pale with round eyes and a crooked stitched mouth. It's a scarecrow, a boy, and I can just make out two wings sprouting from his back.

"Crowky," I say, the name coming easily to my lips. I stare at his black button eyes and his smile seems to stretch.

"I'd almost forgotten about you," I whisper.

CHAPTER 4

After lunch Rose disappears to our room, and Grandad comes up to the attic to check on our progress.

"Carrying all the stuff down the stairs is taking ages," I complain, staggering under a pile of magazines. "We need a quicker way."

Grandad looks out of the attic window. "Maybe you could use this."

I join him and I see that the garden is directly below us. "I suppose we could lower everything down on a rope. . . ."

"Or maybe," Grandad says, grabbing a handful of my magazines, "you could chuck it all out!" And before I can say, *no, that's a ridiculous idea*, he's hurled the magazines out of the window. They flutter through the air and land all over the grass. He turns to me with a gleam in his eye. "Your turn, Arthur!"

"Isn't it a bit dangerous?"

"Not if we only do the small stuff. And no glass or metal, right?"

"Right," I agree, nodding seriously. Then, with a yell, I hurl out the rest of the magazines, making Grandad laugh with glee.

Then we get down to the serious business of throwing the contents of the attic out of the window. We go into a bit of a frenzy, whooping and yelling as bags burst open midair and boxes explode on the patio.

Eventually, and predictably, Rose comes up to ruin our fun.

"Grandad, your underpants are hanging in a tree!" she cries. "Why have you even kept them?"

"I was saving them to use as dusters," he explains, then, possibly because Rose looks so disgusted, he shuffles off to collect them, coughing all the way down the stairs.

"Inhaler!" Rose and I call after him. Then Rose flops down on the sofa, pulls a piano keyboard onto her lap, and starts randomly pressing the keys.

"Do you want to chuck some stuff out?" I ask, hauling a bag toward the window. "This one's full of cuddly toys."

"Nah."

So, while Rose's creepy music fills the attic, I throw the cuddly toys out. Grandad appears and tries to catch them. When a stuffed Winnie the Pooh hits him in the face he starts to fight it. It's really funny. I turn around to tell Rose to come and watch, but then I change my mind. There's no way she's getting off that sofa.

Rose used to be all right. No, she was better than all right.

She was funny and laughed at my jokes and, except for the dark, she wasn't scared of anything. It was Rose who jumped off the harbor wall one summer, right in front of all those teenage boys, and Rose who worked out that we could sled down the sand dunes on trays. At school we were in the same class and played together every recess. I thought Rose liked this as much as I did, until our principal decided to mix up the Year Five classes.

We were given a piece of paper and told to write down the names of three people we wanted to be with. I wrote down one name: *Rose*. I didn't need anyone else. But then our teacher left the pieces of paper on his desk and I saw Rose's list. She'd written:

Angel

Nisha

Briony

Rose was really happy in her class with her three friends. Across the corridor, I wasn't so happy. Then Rose got her phone and got into YouTube, makeup, and her mates, and the Rose I knew just sort of disappeared.

I turn back to the window and shake out the last of the toys. Grandad is lying flat on his back now, letting them fall all over him. After the last teddy has bounced off his stomach I go to clear out the darkest corner of the attic.

I push aside a chunky TV and find myself staring into the sparkly eyes of a rocking horse. It rocks slightly, eyes wide, teeth bared, as if it's angry about being left in this dingy spot for so long.

I grab its mane and pull it out. "Look who I've found, Rose!"

She looks up. "What? It's just the old rocking horse."

"Yes, but it's *your* old rocking horse, isn't it? It was you who painted it black and covered it in glitter, and then you said it belonged to you and I was never allowed to sit on it. What did you call it?"

"Orion," she says flatly. "You'd better put it in the thrift shop pile. Someone might want it."

Suddenly I want to make Rose admit that she used to love this rocking horse. I want her to look at it, and be interested in it, and stop being cool, just for a second. . . .

"Hey, Rose." I drag it toward the window. "Do you think Orion would like to fly?"

She looks up. "What're you on about?"

"He's been stuck in the attic for too long. I think he'd like to feel the wind beneath his hooves." I'm at the window now.

She leaps off the sofa and grabs hold of the mane. "You can't throw him out of the window, Arthur. He's an antique!"

"He?" I say. "*He?*"

Rose narrows her eyes.

"Do you think you can you still talk to *him*, Rose?"

She yanks the rocking horse out of my hands. "Let's see, shall we?" Then she crouches down and presses her ear to his mouth. "What was that, Orion? Uh-huh. Got it." She looks up. "Orion wants me to tell you that you smell like the corridor outside the boys' toilets. In fact, Orion thinks that the corridor outside the boys' toilets might actually smell *of Arthur*." She smiles sweetly. "It looks like I can still talk to him!"

"Yeah? Well, maybe I can too." I stick my ear next to its mouth. "Sorry, Orion? You think Rose's perfume smells like cat poo after it's been in the sun? OK, I'll pass it on."

Now it's Rose's turn. She rams her ear against his mouth. "Uh-huh, yep, got it." She looks up. "What Orion *actually* said was that it's you who smells like cat poo after it's been in the sun. You got it wrong because, unlike me, you don't speak fluent Moonlight Stallion."

Moonlight Stallion. Ha! I knew Rose was still into Orion! He used to pop up in loads of our games and I'm sure she was always sitting on him when we played Roar.

Roar. In a flash it's back, and an image darts into my mind of Rose sitting high on Orion, bossing me around and translating his insults for me.

Orion rocks forward and again I feel like he's looking at me. I tug him toward the window by his tail, suddenly desperate to get away from his sparkly staring eyeballs. "He still wants to fly," I say. "He said so."

Rose's hands grab the tail. "I'd let go of that if I were you."

"Why?"

Her voice drops to a dramatic whisper. "Because since you last saw Orion his tail has become *poisonous* and every single strand stings like a bee. The pain is intense, Arthur, and it will shoot through you like a thousand needles burrowing into your skin!"

"So? You're holding the tail too!"

She shoves her face close to mine, eyes shining, and whispers, "The poison only affects BOYS!"

A chuckle makes us look up. Grandad is standing in the doorway with a cup of coffee. "It's so wonderful to see you two playing again. Nothing could make me happier."

"We're not playing, Grandad." Rose lets go of Orion's tail. "We're *fighting*. Big difference."

"Sounded a bit like playing to me," he says, then he sits on the sofa, props his feet on a suitcase, and says, "Well, get on with it. This attic won't clear itself out."

CHAPTER 5

It's fun having Grandad in the attic. He plays tunes on the keyboard and seems excited by everything we find.

Grandad and Nani grew up in Mauritius, and when I discover something I think came from there I show it to him: an empty bottle of Labourdonnais rum, one of Nani's old saris, a tin that once contained Bois Cheri tea.

"I can smell home," says Grandad, sticking his nose in the tin and breathing deeply.

All this nostalgia makes Grandad move on to singing sea shanties in French, and Rose and I fall quiet as his deep voice fills the room. We've only visited Mauritius once, when we were little, and I can hardly remember it. I can hardly remember Nani either. She died when we were three. Rose and I start to put anything that might have belonged to Nani on the sofa next to Grandad. He glances down at the beads and scarves and boxes, but he doesn't stop singing until Rose pulls a half-deflated dinghy into the middle of the room.

It's not the dinghy that interests him, but something hidden behind it.

He disappears into the shadows of the eaves and comes back dragging a cot. "Remember this old thing?" he asks.

It's an ancient cot, one of those ones on wheels that folds in the middle, like a table-tennis table. It has a moldy-looking orange mattress, rusty springs, and a plastic headboard. . . . It's rubbish, but just looking at it makes my heart beat fast because Rose and I loved playing with it. We kept it closed, and the folded mattress made a damp, dark tunnel that we would dare each other to crawl through. I can clearly remember the spine-tingling feeling I got when I pushed my head inside and forced myself to go into the darkness.

"Arthur peed in that," says Rose.

"I did not! I spilled a juice box in there."

"Whatever," she says with an infuriating smile.

Grandad runs his hand through the dust on the headboard. "Well, one of you definitely did something to it. Look at this!"

I see some words are scratched into the plastic headboard.

"'Enter here for the Land of Roar,'" I read, although what it actually says is,

ENTUR HEER FOR THE LANED OF ROAR!!!

I slip my hand into my pocket and touch the corner of the map.

"What's the Land of Roar?" asks Grandad.

"Just some game we used to play," says Rose.

Suddenly I know exactly why we scratched those words onto the headboard. "This was how we got there," I say. "We'd crawl into the bed, shout 'Hear me roar,' and when we came out the other side we'd be in Roar!"

Rose groans. "We'd be in *the attic*, Arthur."

"I know," I say quickly. "I mean, it's how the game always began."

Grandad pats the bed. "Well, how about it, twins? Fancy crawling through the bed and having one last adventure in Roar?"

Rose looks at him in horror. "Grandad, we haven't played games like that for years. Plus I'm not going anywhere near that stinky old pee mattress." She gives the bed a shake. "It's heavy. Do you want me to help you get it downstairs so we can bring it to the dump?"

"No," I say quickly. "We're saving the big stuff for the end. Right, Grandad?"

He nods. "But I have seen one big thing we can get rid of." He picks up the dinghy and carries it toward the window. "Let's see how far this baby can fly!"

He forces it halfway out, then gives it a massive shove. Rose and I get to the window just in time to see the dinghy float over the garden wall and land on the Baileys' conservatory.

"Oh dear," says Grandad. "I suppose I'd better get it back."

"I'll go," cries Rose, dashing out of the attic.

Soon I see Rose run outside, climb on the rubbish bin, and scramble into next door's garden. Mazen is on her trampoline; she acknowledges Rose's presence by shrieking, "What *are* you wearing?" then doing a backflip.

"Well, Arthur?" Grandad is watching me. "Are you up for taking one last trip to Roar?"

Honestly? I'd give anything to play Roar with Rose again. Just me and her, and a load of dragons and unicorns and no thoughts of starting secondary school. But it's impossible. I'm too old and I couldn't do it without her. The rush of excitement that I felt when I saw the bed has gone and in its place is a heavy lump of disappointment. "No thanks, Grandad. Rose is right. We don't play games like that anymore."

Outside, we can hear Rose and Mazen talking, then the squeak of trampoline springs.

"Who said anything about playing a game?" Grandad grins, then turns away. "Come on. I saw a bag of tennis balls earlier. Let's see if we can chuck them as far as Mazen's trampoline."

CHAPTER 6

B y the end of the day the attic is empty.

Well, almost. The cot is sitting in the middle of the room, watched over by Orion, but everything else has gone: the dressing-up clothes, the plastic weapons, the Playmobil, the cuddly toys. Even the candy tin is down in the garden in the dump pile.

I take one last look around the room, and turn out the light.

Grandad seems to have forgotten about the meal commonly known as dinner, so Rose and I heat up a pizza we find at the bottom of the freezer, then put ourselves to bed. We have to. It's midnight and Grandad is out in the garden, dancing around a bonfire he's made out of old newspapers and egg boxes.

The pizza and trampolining have put Rose in a good mood because she starts kicking the bottom of my bunk bed, distracting me from the book I'm reading. The only downside to staying at Grandad's is having to share a room with Rose.

Eventually the kicking stops and I try to get into my book. Clearing out the attic has left me feeling a bit weird and on edge, but soon I find myself pulled into the story. It's about a girl who discovers she's descended from a samurai warrior and can defeat any enemy by summoning the ghost of her ancestor. I wouldn't be worried about starting secondary school if I had a samurai ghost on my side.

Rose's voice drifts up from the bottom bunk. "Arthur . . . Mazen says you're going to be eaten alive at Langton Academy."

Some people believe that twins can read each other's minds. I can't read Rose's mind, but sometimes she can read mine.

"Mazen says, because you can't play football and you got a telescope instead of a phone for your birthday, everyone will think you're weird."

I really don't like Mazen Bailey.

"Oh, and Mazen says you should use product on your hair. To make it, you know, less big or people will laugh at you."

Actually I think I might hate Mazen Bailey.

"Arthur? Can you hear me?" Rose gives the bottom of the bed an extra big kick. "Mazen was only trying to help. She's in Year Eight so she knows."

"Mazen Bailey," I say, after a moment of dignified silence, "believes that *The Force Awakens* is the first Star Wars film, so obviously her opinion counts for nothing."

Rose goes quiet and all I can hear is tap, tap, tap, tap.

"Rose, are you sending her a message?"

"Shh," she says. "Did you just say *obviously* her opinion counts for nothing, or *clearly* her opinion counts for nothing?"

I throw myself over the side of the bunk bed and make a grab for Rose's phone, but she just pushes me away and keeps typing. "Rose, if you press send I'll—"

She looks up, interested. "Yes? What will you do?"

"I'll . . . I'll . . ." What can I do? What power do I have over Rose these days? She doesn't want to hang out with me. I don't make her laugh anymore. Everything about me annoys her. "I won't sleep in here!" I shout.

She bursts out laughing. "So? That would be great!" Then she presses her finger down. "Oops . . . I just pressed send!"

Rage surges through me and I badly want to hit Rose, but I can't, because she's my sister and hitting my sister when I was six might have been just about OK, but hitting my sister when I'm eleven is wrong.

Rose laughs. "You look funny, Arthur. Are you going to cry?"

Over my dead body, I think, but I do have a painful lump in my throat because what Rose just did was so disloyal. Rose and I are twins. We're supposed to stick together!

The lump in my throat gets bigger and I have to squeeze my eyes shut to make it go away.

"You are," Rose says confidently. "You're going to cry."

But I don't cry. Instead I do the thing I always do when

there's a *chance* I might cry. "ARRRGHHHH!" I scream in her face. Then I grab my duvet and stomp out of the room, slamming the door behind me.

No way am I sleeping in the same room as my disloyal, evil, mocking sister. No way am I ever speaking to her again. No way am I even going to breathe the same air that she breathes. . . .

There's just one problem.

Where can I sleep?

Grandad's house is big, but it's also full. There are two spare bedrooms, but neither of them has beds. One of them has got Grandad's drum kit in it, and the other's full of books and Nani's old things. Then I remember where there's a perfectly good bed. One that folds in the middle and has a mattress covered in orange and brown flowers and *Entur heer for the laned of ROAR!!!* scratched into the headboard.

A bed that I'm ninety-nine percent certain I didn't pee in.

CHAPTER 7

It turns out attics, especially empty ones, are extremely creepy at night.

Moonlight streams in through the single window, lighting up the cot and making Orion look extra glittery. I step inside, my duvet trailing behind me, and flick on the light switch.

Nothing happens.

It takes several more pushes before I realize the bulb must have gone. It doesn't matter. I'm going to sleep. I don't need a light to open up a cot and fall asleep.

And yet . . . it is *very* shadowy up here, and quiet, and Orion's silver eyeballs are staring right at me. I take a step to the left. Orion's still staring at me. Step to the right. He's still staring. This is stupid. Orion can't stare. He's made of wood and doesn't have functioning eyeballs, and Orion is not a *he*: Orion is an *it*, an inanimate object!

That for some reason is rocking ever so slightly.

I'm about to step forward when I have the uncanny feeling that someone, or something, is up here in the attic with me.

Immediately I think of the shadow I saw at the window, the wizard, and for a second I actually feel weak at the knees. So I decide to do what Dad says he does whenever he feels scared. I laugh out loud.

"Ha ha ha ha!"

Wow. Dad is so wrong about that.

I tell myself that it's my mind playing tricks on me again, then I put my shoulders back and walk toward the cot. I'm a step away when I hear a tiny fluttering sound. I freeze and hold my breath and listen. I hear it again. It sounds like wings brushing against something, and wings remind me of the map, and of the wild-looking face grinning at me from the window of the Crow's Nest.

Crowky.

I've thought a lot about Crowky since I found the map. It was Rose who invented him out of the two things I hated most in the world: scarecrows and crows.

My scarecrow fear began when I once got lost in a corn maze. I'd run on ahead of my family and suddenly realized I was all on my own. Except for the scarecrows, and they were everywhere. I ran around a corner and saw a policeman scarecrow; I ran left and saw a Father Christmas scarecrow. I was about to start screaming when I spotted Mum on the next path. "Mum!" I shouted, forcing my way toward her and grabbing the sleeve of her denim jacket. Then her arm fell off.

It wasn't Mum. It was an Elvis scarecrow, and that's when I started screaming.

I swear to this day that their jackets were identical.

I'd have probably gotten over the scarecrow thing if, later in the day, Rose hadn't thought it would be funny to feed some birds by sprinkling crumbs in my hair. A crow landed on my head and got a bit stuck, and the next time we were in Grandad's attic Rose came up with Crowky. She could do his voice really well, all scratchy and wicked. "*I'm going to get you, Arthur Trout!*" she'd rasp, filling me with dread. "*I'm going to get yooooou!*"

And it's exactly that dread I'm feeling right now as I stand as still as possible, hardly daring to breathe, listening to every sound.

A pipe gurgles. The window rattles in its frame. Outside, Grandad's bonfire crackles. Then I hear it: a violent, wild fluttering as if something huge and feathery is trapped *inside* the cot.

I turn and run for the door.

Rose, I decide, is forgiven.

CHAPTER 8

"Arthur, are you telling me you're scared of a cot?"

Rose's laughter floats up to me as I stare at the ceiling, for once pleased that the room is lit by her stupid rabbit night-light.

"Not the *cot*," I say, "Something *inside* it. It sounded like feathers. There must be a bird stuck in there."

Down on the bottom bunk, Rose snorts. "We were in the attic all afternoon. I think we'd have noticed a bird flying around."

"But it's not flying around, is it? It's *in* the bed."

"Maybe, or maybe you're scared of the cot. I mean, you're scared of lots of things, Arthur: scarecrows, crows, frogs—"

"Says the girl who has to sleep with a night-light."

Rose ignores me and carries on—"Mushrooms, substitute teachers, starting at Langton Academy, heights, Mum's black pointy shoes, fire, raisins with stalks—"

"I don't *like* raisins with stalks, but I'm not scared of them, or any of those other things. When my class made a scarecrow I sewed on its button eyes and it didn't bother me at all." It did. A bit. "Plus I was scared of Mum's shoes when I was, like, two, not now. In fact," I declare boldly, "right now I can't think of a single thing I'm scared of."

"Oh really?" Then everything goes quiet on the bottom bunk. A bit too quiet. When Rose speaks, her voice is as scratchy as a nail being dragged down a wall. *"What about ME, Arthur Trout? Are you scared of ME?"* I might not have heard her Crowky voice for a long time, but I'd recognize it anywhere. It actually makes me need to pee. That's how good it is.

"Rose, I thought you said you couldn't remember Roar? Because that's where Crowky came from."

Silence. Then the scratchy voice says, *"Rose isn't here anymore, Arthur. It's just you and me. Now will you admit that you're just a teeny bit scared of me?"*

And that's when I think of a brilliant way to get back at Rose, for the voice, for messaging Mazen, for calling me a loser, for *everything*.

"I am a bit," I say, "but not as scared as you are of . . . THE DARK." I lean over the side of the bunk bed, grab Rose's rabbit night-light, and switch it off. Rose's response is creative, fast, and totally unexpected. She jumps out of bed, climbs the ladder, and throws a cup of water in my face.

"Rose!" I shout.

"HA!" she screams back.

Outside in the garden, Grandad yodels.

CHAPTER 9

Next morning, I eat my Crunchy Nut cornflakes sitting on the sofa in the garden. It was the last thing we dragged out of the attic and now it's wedged between the patio and the plum tree and covered in ash from Grandad's bonfire.

The sky is blue and the sun is shining. A blackbird hops around in the bushes. It seems like a totally normal day, but I don't feel normal. I drink the sugary milk from the bottom of the bowl. I feel jittery and uneasy and I can't stop looking up at the attic window.

Grandad wanders out of the house and blinks into the sunshine. He's wearing a cardigan, an old T-shirt—the one that says "NO PROB-LLAMA!"—and his painting shorts. "Hello, mate," he says. "Where's your sister?"

I nod toward the neighbor's garden. Rose's head appears above the wall, then disappears. There's a squeak of trampoline springs, then her head pops back up, her hair flying out straight and long.

"Rose, you're not doing it right!" cries Mazen. "You look like there's something wrong with you!"

"Not got anything to do?" says Grandad. "Rose doesn't fancy going to the beach?"

"No. All Rose wants to do is jump and look at her phone." I think back to the damp night's sleep I've just had. "Right now Rose hates me and I hate her."

"You *hate* each other?" Grandad chuckles. "You two have always gotten along fine."

He's wrong. We *used* to get along fine until Rose changed into that stranger I can see on the trampoline. But I don't bother telling Grandad this. Instead I say, "Last night we had a fight."

"That's normal. I remember your mum and Jack fighting like mad when they were little. They used to draw blood."

"Jack was a cat, Grandad."

"I know, but the point is they'd be cuddling on the sofa by bedtime."

"I'm fairly certain me and Rose won't be doing any cuddling ever again."

He laughs and ruffles my hair. "Come on. While you're waiting for Rose to stop hating you, we can get the cot down from the attic."

I get up, glance once more at the attic window, then with a heavy and slightly scared heart I follow Grandad back inside the house.

It's amazing what a positive effect sunlight can have on

a room. If I ignore Orion glaring at me from the corner, there is almost nothing spooky about the attic right now.

Grandad grabs hold of the cot and starts to heave. "I got this thing up here, so presumably I can get it down again. Do you think we should chuck it out of the window?"

"Better not. It might kill Rose."

He laughs. "See? I knew you didn't hate her! Now get over here and give me a hand."

But I don't move. Instead I just stand in the doorway, staring at the grubby old cot, which was the start of the best game I ever played, a game that until yesterday I'd almost forgotten.

"Unless . . . ," says Grandad, "you think we should leave the bed up here?"

Yes, I want to say, *leave it up here and let's bring the swords and dressing-up clothes back up too.* But what would be the point? Rose is never going to play Roar or any other game with me. "No," I say. "It's time to chuck it out." Then I grab the other side of the bed and start pushing.

We've only moved it a couple of meters before Grandad has to stop to catch his breath. We rest against the cot while he has a puff on his inhaler. "Arthur," he says, "do you remember when you had a funny turn up here?"

I think for a moment. "When I was crawling through the cot?"

"That's it! I came in and found you curled up on the floor. You had two teeth marks on your wrist." He points just below my hand at the pale scar I've had for as long as I can remember. "Rose said a dragon had bitten you, but I'm guessing she was the dragon?" Grandad watches me, waiting for an answer.

It must have been Rose who bit me that day . . . so when I look at my wrist why do I remember my fingers touching rough scales, then hearing a warning growl followed by a flash of movement, and then the shock of sharp teeth grazing my skin?

With a start, I realize that this is what my memories of Roar are like. When I think about Win and Mitch, I don't see me and Rose running around the attic talking to invisible mermaids and pretend ninja-wizards. I see a real girl swimming below the surface of clear water, her thick tail flicking from side to side, and a real boy sitting by a fire. The boy has wonky teeth and he's grinning at me from under a wizard's hat.

I take a deep breath. "It wasn't Rose who bit me . . ."

Grandad turns to look at me. "Who was it, then?"

I rub the pale scar, trying to decide whether to carry on talking or shut up. But I can't keep quiet. Everything that has happened since we arrived at Grandad's is too strange. I have to tell someone.

"I was standing by a dragon." My voice is loud in the

silence of the attic. "The dragon had scales and chipped claws and smoke pouring out of its nose, and even though Rose told me not to, I brushed my fingers along its belly, and then . . ." I look at Grandad. "It bit me."

Grandad has an unusual expression on his face—one that I've hardly ever seen before. He looks serious.

"Grandad, why aren't you laughing and telling me I'm talking rubbish?"

He smiles and shrugs. "Because I believe you."

Everything has gone quiet: the birds outside, even Rose and Mazen on the trampoline. The sun shines down on my legs and something warm, like magic, creeps through me. "What do you mean?"

He laughs. "Just what I said, Arthur: I believe you!"

Grandad is winding me up. He loves playing tricks on us—he loves playing full stop—and this is just another of his games. And yet . . . *I know* I saw a shadow at the window and heard the wings fluttering in the bed.

Just thinking about the wings makes my heart speed up. I jump up and look at the bed.

"What's wrong, Arthur?" Grandad clambers to his feet.

"Yesterday I heard something coming from in there." I can't take my eyes off the bed. "It made me think of someone in Roar."

"A bad person?"

I nod. "A very bad person."

"And you think this person might be in the bed?" Again I nod. Grandad puts his arm around me and pulls me close. His cardigan feels soft against my face. It smells of coffee and his shed. "Well, there's one way to find out, Arthur. You need to crawl into the bed."

CHAPTER 10

I stare at the sagging mattress, then back at Grandad. "What? You think I should just crawl in there?"

Grandad nods. "And visit Roar." He says this like he's suggesting a trip to the pier.

"But Grandad, Roar was *a game*. Remembering a dragon biting me is my mind playing tricks on me."

"But what if it's not, Arthur? What if you and Rose made Roar with your imaginations, then crawled through the cot and somehow found your way there?"

I smile and shake my head. "If I crawl into that mattress, I'll come straight out the other side and you'll be standing there laughing at me!"

"Well, if that happens, at least you know you imagined the funny sound and being bitten by a dragon, and can get on with turning this attic into a den."

"And if I do end up in Roar?"

I can't believe these words have just come out of my mouth.

Grandad's eyes go wide. "Now wouldn't that be something?" And then he actually holds the mattress open for me and says, "In you go!"

"I don't know." I glance out of the window to make sure Rose is still on the trampoline. There aren't many things in the world she'd find more hilarious than the sight of me crawling through the cot trying to get to Roar. There she is, jumping up and down and trying to touch her toes. "I'm sure I imagined it," I say. "It was probably a bird in the chimney or—"

A scuffle makes me turn around and I see that Grandad's head and shoulders are stuck inside the mattress. *What is he doing?* He must think that if he goes in first, I'll follow. He pushes in his arms and then starts wriggling from side to side, trying to get his bum in too. Then I hear a faint cry of "Hear me roar!"

The sight of a seventy-two-year-old man attempting to squeeze his body into a folded cot is like a slap in the face. What am I doing? Rose is right. I'm way too old for this. I should be learning to surf, or skating, or fighting stuff on the computer. *Anything* would be better than playing in the attic with my grandad!

When Grandad comes out the other side of the bed I'll tell him I want to take the cot to the dump. It's time for me to grow up, or I really will be eaten alive at secondary school.

"Hear me *ROOOOOAAAAR!*" Grandad cries, then with a final lurch he gets his bum and legs into the bed too. Then he just sits there, a big bulge in the middle of the mattress. It reminds me of the time I saw a nature documentary about a snake that had swallowed a pig. It's pretty funny actually.

"All right, Grandad. You can come out now." I try to give the bed a shake but it weighs a ton with him in there.

Grandad's hand pops out and waves around.

"Are you stuck?" I grab hold of his hand and his fingers wrap around my wrist and I start to pull. But he won't budge, and now I'm laughing because Grandad has got me to play, just like he wanted to. "Come on. I might have peed in there, remember?"

Suddenly Grandad's fingers tighten around mine. "Ow!" I say, still laughing. Then I sit down on the floor, put my feet against the bed, and pull as hard as I can. But Grandad doesn't budge and his big hand squeezes even tighter around mine. In fact, his fingers are going white from the pressure and my hand starts to hurt. "Grandad, stop it!" Panic rises up in me as the pressure increases. It feels like the bones in my fingers might break!

I pull harder than ever, but I'm not trying to get Grandad out: I'm trying to free my hand. "Grandad, you're hurting me!"

Suddenly he lets go and I tumble backward. Then, with amazing speed, his hand shoots inside the mattress. *What?* I cradle my squashed hand to my chest and stare at the bed. The lump has gone!

"Grandad?" I jump to my feet and circle the bed, patting the springs. "Grandad? Where are you?"

Silence. My heart thuds against my rib cage. I grab the headboard, ready to pull the bed open . . . but something stops me. It's the memory of Rose saying, *Never open the cot, Arthur, or everything in Roar will disappear.*

I let go of the headboard. *Rose was talking rubbish,* I tell myself. *There is no Roar; there can't be any Roar.* But I still can't bring myself to open the bed. The attic feels unbearably hot and I'm shaky with panic. I brush a tear off my cheek. "Come on, Grandad . . . It's a good joke, but you can come out now."

I know I'm talking to myself. I know he isn't in there.

In a daze I check every corner of the attic, even under the bed, but except for Orion, the attic is empty. I tell myself that Grandad *has* to be in the bed and I kneel down, take a deep breath, and push my hand into the mattress.

It's horrible. The hairs on the back of my neck prickle as I feel around, desperately hoping that my fingers will touch some bit of Grandad, but my hand just keeps going farther and farther into the mattress until, finally, I do touch something. But it's not Grandad's sneakers or hair. It's a load of spiky, prickly stuff. I grab it and pull it out.

When I uncurl my fingers I have to squeeze my mouth shut to stop myself from being sick. I'm holding a pile of yellow straw and greasy black feathers. I chuck the whole lot on the floor, then reach forward and pick up the largest feather. It's inky black and the quill is sharp and warm, as if moments ago it was attached to a living thing.

A living thing with wings and stuffed full of straw.

I jump to my feet. I have to tell Rose!

CHAPTER 11

As I walk across the garden—my heart still thudding in my chest and my hands trembling—I wonder how I'm going to do this. I can hear Mazen's voice, shrieking at Rose and bossing her around. If I just say what happened, they're going to collapse with laughter. Mazen is going to think I'm sad or crazy, or both. I pull myself onto the rubbish bin. *It doesn't matter*, I tell myself. What matters is that Grandad is missing. I've just got to tell Rose and then she will help me find him.

I look over the wall. Mazen is standing with her hands on her hips, watching Rose. She senses my presence and her head swivels around like a velociraptor. She gives me a long, hard look, then turns back to Rose. "It's your brother," she says.

Rose lands on her bum, then bounces back to her feet. "What do you want, Arthur?"

I cling to the top of the wall. "I need to speak to you."

"Go on then."

"Not here." My eyes flick to Mazen. "On our own."

Rose rolls her eyes. "Just tell me, Arthur."

"Grandad's disappeared!" I say in a rush.

"Grandad's *what?*"

"He's *disappeared*. One second he was in the attic, and the next he was gone. Please stop bouncing, Rose. Grandad's gone and you've got to help me find him!"

With a sigh she comes to a stop.

Mazen stretches, then says, "He's probably lost in all the mess he keeps up there."

"All his 'mess' is in the garden. There's nowhere to get lost in the attic now!"

Mazen shrugs. "Just saying. He's a messy person."

"He's not messy. He's . . . a collector!"

"He's messy, Arthur," snaps Rose, hands on her hips. "Now hurry up and tell me what happened."

"Grandad crawled through the cot—"

"*What?* Why would he do that?"

"It doesn't matter *why* he did it; what matters is that he crawled into the middle of the mattress, then disappeared!"

Rose doesn't look worried or shocked; in fact, she bursts out laughing. "Arthur, he's playing a trick on you!"

Anger rises up inside me. Every second I stand here talking to Rose is another second that Grandad is missing. "He's not. I was holding his hand. I felt him being pulled into the bed. I saw his hand shoot inside!"

"Then he must still be there."

"He isn't. I checked!"

She rolls her eyes. "Well, check again."

I reach into my pocket and feel the feathers and straw that I picked up before I ran out of the attic. "There's something else. . . ." I lean over the wall and open my hand. "I found this inside the bed seconds after Grandad disappeared."

Rose takes a step closer and alarm flashes across her face. "*Crowky* . . . ," she whispers, but then she shakes her head. "It's Grandad. He must have put them there."

"Really? Because I've never told Grandad about Crowky. Have you?"

"What *are* you two talking about?" interrupts Mazen.

"It's nothing," says Rose. "Just Arthur trying to get me to play with him."

I'm so angry I throw the feathers and straw in her face, and Mazen screams, "Get that gross stuff off my trampoline!"

Rose gathers it up and chucks it back at me. "Leave me alone, Arthur! Why can't you accept that I don't want to hang out with you?"

My foot slips out from under me. "Do you honestly think I've made all this up so that you'll spend time with me?"

"*Yes*," she says, making Mazen laugh.

"Well, guess what, Rose? I don't even like you much these days, and I'm only talking to you right now because Grandad has vanished and I think Crowky has got him!"

Now both of them are laughing.

"Fine," I say, my cheeks burning. "If you won't help me, I'll just have to find him on my own." I jump off the rubbish bin, slip on a rotten crab apple, scramble to my feet, then stride toward the back door.

"When you get to Roar, say hi to Mitch!" Rose shouts.

I turn around. Rose is watching me with a sarcastic smile on her face.

"You've changed so much Mitch wouldn't even recognize you," I say. Then I walk into the house and let the door slam shut behind me.

CHAPTER 12

Back in the attic, I stare at the cot.

I've looked for Grandad everywhere. Even though I know he couldn't have gotten out of the bed, I've still checked every room in the house, the cellar, the shed, and even the garage, and opening the bed isn't an option. Some truly weird stuff has happened in the past hour and I'm not about to do anything that might permanently erase my grandad.

He disappeared inside the mattress so that's where I've got to go too.

Trying to ignore the feathers and scraps of straw, I get down on my hands and knees, then push my head inside the bed. I want to pull it straight back out, but I keep my eyes squeezed shut and wriggle farther in. "Hear me roar," I blurt, pulling my legs up behind me. The bed wobbles, then becomes still.

I'm crouched in the middle of the mattress, surrounded by darkness. It feels damp and lumpy and it smells like the PE cupboard at school. The springs from the mattress dig into my skin and I can't find enough air to breathe. All I want to do is get out, but I force myself to stay where I am while I wait for something to happen.

When Rose and I played Roar I'm sure this was when the game began. I don't know how it worked, but when we came out the other side we'd be in Roar. I crouch there, the mattress pressing into my face, until I can't stand it any longer. I crawl forward, my head bursts out into bright light, and I gulp fresh air.

I see dusty floorboards and straw and feathers. Outside, the sun is shining and I can hear Mazen Bailey laughing. I pull myself all the way out of the bed, feeling relieved and scared and stupid, all at the same time, then I walk back around to the other side of the bed.

Grandad is still missing and I'm going to keep crawling through this mattress until I find him.

And for the next ten minutes that's exactly what I do.

Soon my eyes are itchy, I'm sweaty, and my hair is massive and crackling with static.

I'm wriggling onto the attic floor for the thirty-second time when I see Rose standing in the doorway, sucking a blue ice pop and watching me.

"I've looked for him everywhere," I say. "This is the only thing left to do."

She does a long hard suck on the ice pop, then says, "I'll admit it's strange that he's vanished."

I'm so relieved to hear her say this that I jump to my feet

and rush over. "I told you: Grandad's vanished inside the bed and somehow we've got to go there, go to Roar, and get him back!"

She sighs. "Arthur, we never actually *went* to Roar. You know that, right? The whole time we were playing up here in the attic, pretending."

"But when we played Roar, it didn't feel like we were in the attic. It felt *real*."

All the time I've been talking Rose has been sucking hard on her ice pop, draining all the blue out of it. "I suppose it felt different to other games," she admits. "But do you remember when I said I could fly? I got you all to come and watch, and it turned out it was just me jumping down the stairs flapping my arms." She shrugs. "Kids have got big imaginations."

"That's exactly what I thought, before I felt Grandad being pulled into the bed!" I show her the marks on my hand where Grandad's nails dug in. "And there's another thing. . . . Just before he disappeared Grandad basically said he believed that Roar was real."

Rose laughs. "Arthur, this whole thing is a massive practical joke! I bet Grandad's had this planned for ages."

"Grandad would never scare me like this."

She raises one eyebrow. "Wouldn't he?"

"No, he wouldn't!"

Rose shrugs like she couldn't care less what I think. "Suit yourself. I'm going to town. Mazen says there's a three-for-two sale on at Claire's. Before I went I thought I should check that you hadn't vanished too."

And that's when I realize it's hopeless. If Rose is more bothered about hair bands and earrings than she is about Grandad, I don't want her to come with me. "Fine." I walk back to the cot, crouch down, and roll up my sleeves. "Hear me roar," I mutter as I stick my head back into the mattress.

"Hah!" says Rose.

I pull my head out and turn to look at her, eyes narrowed. I am in no mood to hear Rose's sarcastic hahs. "What?"

"Nothing. . . . Only I never said, 'Hear me roar' because even when I was five I thought it was stupid. When I got into the middle of the mattress I just shut my eyes and imagined Roar, then when I came out the other side I was there." She takes a last long suck on her ice pop, then turns to the door. "See you later, loser."

CHAPTER 13

I pull my legs in behind me and I crouch in the middle of the bed, just like before.

Only this time I don't bother with any magic words. Instead I use Rose's technique: I close my eyes and I imagine Roar.

It's hard to begin with. Roar is buried at the back of my mind. Some details like Win's hat and Crowky's voice are crystal clear, but most of it is hazy and muddled, like my memories of Nani and the first house we ever lived in.

But then something comes back to me. The feeling of holding a soft creature in my hands. This thing has got wings and they're batting against my fingers. *Furry.* I'm holding a furry. I'm not sure exactly what a furry is, but suddenly I know there were loads of them in Roar.

Then my mind is full of fuzzies—I see them hovering like dragonflies and sunbathing on stones, and Roar comes rushing back to me as fast as the fuzzies' beating wings.

I see me and Win standing on a ship—the *Raven*—and I feel the spray from the Bottomless Ocean stinging my eyes. I hear a shout to my left—"Get back! Before he burns your hair off!" and I turn to see Rose tossing bits of doughnut to a hovering dragon.

Crowky lands with a thump on the deck of the *Raven*. His black wings billow around him like a cloud as he grabs hold of my arm and hisses, *"I've got you now, Arthur Trout!"*

Keeping my eyes squeezed shut and my mind stuffed full of Roar, I start to crawl farther into the mattress. Left hand, right hand. I see Mitch—her blue hair trailing behind her, tangled and encrusted with shells. Left hand, right hand. I smell the bonfire and popcorn smell of Wininja's cave. Left hand, right hand. Somewhere at the back of my brain I register that I should have fallen onto the attic floor by now, and that this is taking far too long, but I push the thought away and picture Roar's night sky crammed so full of stars it looked like a bag of glitter had been thrown across black velvet.

There were millions of stars in Roar—blue, green, pink, purple—and their light was as warm as the sun. Those stars used to shine down on me and Rose when we were floating in Mitch's lagoon. They made patterns on our skin.

I freeze, snapping back to where I am. But something has changed. My hands aren't pressing into a soft and spongy mattress anymore. They're touching something cold and hard. Holding my breath, I feel around. The mattress has gone. I'm kneeling on stone!

Icy fear rushes through me. This is what I wanted to happen, wasn't it? I wanted to crawl into the cot and for something magical to happen, but now that rock is digging into my hands and knees, I'm so scared that my whole body is shaking.

I force myself to open my eyes. Thick blackness surrounds me, but far ahead I can just make out a tiny pinprick of green light. And the air isn't dusty anymore. It's cool and damp, and I can hear rushing water.

I start to crawl toward the green light. My head scrapes against the roof of the tunnel and rocks graze my hands, but I don't stop until I reach the very end and the green light has become a curtain of leaves with light shining through

it. Before I can change my mind I push my head through the leaves and crawl out into dazzling sunshine.

I blink and rub my eyes. I'm on a narrow ledge. I lean forward and see that the ledge is set into a cliff and far below me is a deep round pool. Trying to ignore the terrifying drop, I look straight ahead. I'm staring across a valley with a river winding through it. The river passes forests and mountains and glittering lakes. One side of the valley is bright and alive and bursting with leaves and color, while the other half is shadowy and barren. The river has a shifting, swirling rainbow shine on its surface and it leads to a wild sea. Far, far away, beyond the sea, are snow-topped mountains.

Gazing at this unbelievable sight, I should feel lost and scared. But I don't . . . because *this* is Roar.

CHAPTER 14

Everything is quiet and still. The trees, the pool below me, even my breathing.

There's a sudden flash of red feathers as a bird explodes from a tree. It swivels its head in my direction, blinks its beady eyes, then flies away.

I laugh and my voice echoes across the valley. Then I stand up on wobbly legs. The tunnel is behind me and the pool is far below me. But I don't want to think about that. I haven't got a clue how I'm going to get off this ledge. No way am I jumping.

I fumble in my pocket and pull out the map, thinking it might show me a safe way down, but before I can open it the ledge starts to tremble. Seconds later, a loud rumble comes from high above the cliff. Fear flashes through me as the rumble gets louder and the map is whipped from my hands by a sudden gust of wind. I look up just as a wave of water bursts over the top of the cliff and crashes down. *The On-Off Waterfall*, I think as the water smacks into me, knocking me off the ledge. *How could I have forgotten the On-Off Waterfall?*

I somersault through the air before plunging headfirst into cold, deep water.

My breath is punched out of me and water shoots up my nose. I panic, kicking out with my arms and legs, fighting my way up to the surface where I gasp for air.

I'm trying to work out if any of my bones are broken when something closes around me . . . a net! I struggle against the ropes, but they squeeze tight, forcing me into a ball. With a jerk, I'm whipped back up into the air so fast I don't even have time to scream.

The net bounces a few times before coming to a stop. Now I'm dangling over the pool with my arms pinned to my sides and both knees squashed into my chin. Looking up, I see that the net is tied to the thick branch of a tree. With a squeak it begins to turn and I try to work out what on earth— or wherever I am—has just happened to me.

I know that I crawled through the cot, left Grandad's attic, and arrived here. I know my face is stinging from where I smacked into the pool, that my lungs ache from holding my breath, and right now the spinning net is giving me motion-sickness. Could I be in some sort of cot-induced coma? Maybe I had a panic attack in the mattress and passed out?

The net comes to a stop, then starts to turn in the opposite direction. No, this is painfully real. And if I'm trapped like a fly in a web, then it means someone, or something, wants to trap me. My eyes flick to the trees surrounding the pool and my heart speeds up as I try to remember if we ever put any spiders in Roar.

Just then a bloodcurdling scream shatters the silence and a robed, hooded figure leaps from a tree and lands on top of me. Sneakers dig into my face as the figure yells, "SUBMIT OR DIE!" and starts whacking me with a long stick.

No, I think as the stick smacks my legs and I catch a glimpse of silver. Not a stick: *a bokken.* Essentially it's a meter ruler covered in silver foil, and I saw an identical one yesterday in Grandad's attic. I know who that bokken belonged to in Roar: Wininja, my best non-real friend in the world.

"Win, stop it!" I shout. "It's me!"

But he's enjoying himself too much to even hear me. Instead he keeps hitting me and shouting, "SUBMIT OR DIE . . . SUBMIT OR DIE!"

"I submit! I SUBMIT!" *Thwack* goes the bokken right across my fingers. "Ow! Win, stop hitting me. It's me, Arthur Trout!"

Win gasps and the bokken splashes into the pool, then he scampers around the net until we're face-to-face. His head is covered by a ninja hood, but I can still see familiar gray eyes staring back at me. "Arthur . . . Arthur Trout? Master of Roar?" He pokes a finger into my face. "You've come back. I DO NOT believe it!"

"Neither do I," I blurt out. "I didn't think you were real, but here you are: all solid and real, like me . . . or a wall . . . or a tree . . . or a trampoline—"

"What are you on about, Arthur? Of course I'm real . . . And what's a trampoline?"

"It's a . . . bouncy thing that people have in their yard. You jump on them."

Win gasps. "I saw a trampoline yesterday, Arthur, when I came looking for you!"

The shadow at the window. . . . "I knew it was you in Grandad's attic," I say. "No one believed me!"

Win nods eagerly. "That was me! I came to find you. I couldn't believe it when I crawled into that room, looked out of that window, and saw you and Rose!"

"But if you came to find us, why did you go back to Roar?" The net has come to a standstill and is swaying gently over the pool.

"You and Rose said I was never allowed to visit Home, so I stood as still as a statue until you noticed me, then I disappeared back to Roar. I knew you'd understand."

I shake my head. "Win, you should have written a note or something. You seriously freaked me out."

"Yeah, but it worked, didn't it? You're here."

"I think so. . . ."

For a moment we just stare at each other, me curled in a ball and Win clinging to the net, like neither of us can quite believe our eyes.

Suddenly Win says, "Hey, do you like my new hood? Watch." He grabs the top of his hood and pulls it up, making it form a neat wizard's hat. "WIZARD!" he cries, and I get a glimpse of his round cheeks and grin, before he pushes the pointy bit down and his face is hidden again. "*Ninja . . .*" he whispers. Then he pulls the hood up. "WIZARD!" Down it goes. "*Ninja . . .*" Up. "WIZARD!" Down. "*Ninja . . .* WIZARD! . . . *Ninja . . .* WIZARD!"

"Wininja, I get it," I say weakly. "You've got a new wizard-hat-hood thingy, and it's cool, but right now I think I might be sick and I'm struggling to get my head around the fact that I'm actually in Roar."

He nods solemnly. "I know. It's been a long time, and there have been a lot of changes, right? And the biggest change is me. I've buffed up massively. I've been doing ten push-ups a day and eating loads of apples because I've had to get in shape. You see, since you and Rose stopped visiting us, things have gone a bit . . . dodgy."

The net creaks under our combined weight. "What do you mean, dodgy?"

Win sucks in his breath. "First, the unicorns disappeared and then the Lost Girls abandoned their camp. Then the earth wobbles began and sinkholes started opening up and a few weeks ago Roar nearly split in two. Oh, and you hardly ever see fuzzies these days. I reckon loads of them have been eaten."

Now I'm in Roar I can easily remember what fuzzies are:

they're tiny furry fairies, basically mice with wings . . . but with human faces. "The fuzzies have been *eaten*? Who'd want to eat fuzzies?"

"Crowky, and he doesn't do it because they taste nice; he does it for fun. Crowky's changed lots, Arthur. He's gone *nuts*!"

I grip the net. "That's why I'm here. I think my grandad is in Roar. I think Crowky has taken him!"

I'm half expecting Win to laugh or tell me I'm talking rubbish. After all, it was only ever me and Rose who visited Roar. But instead he just nods and says, "Yep. Crowky's got your grandad."

"*What?*" I twist and turn, desperate to escape. "How do you know?"

"He's been sniffing around the waterfall loads recently and going in and out of the tunnel." Win tugs on the ropes of the net. "That's why I set this up: to catch him. When I turned up earlier there were feathers and bits of straw all over the place. It looked like there'd been a pretty serious fight."

I think back to the feathers and straw I found in the cot, and the sounds I heard last night. If Crowky was in the tunnel, maybe he managed to grab hold of Grandad and drag him into Roar. That would explain why it felt like Grandad was yanked out of my hands.

"Oh, and I found this in the mud." Win pulls an object out from his robes and holds it in front of my face. I recognize the blue plastic tube immediately: it's Grandad's asthma inhaler.

I push at the net as hard as I can. "That's medicine and it belongs to my grandad. He's got allergies. Feathers make him really wheezy and Crowky's got those enormous wings. Win, we've got to get that inhaler to Grandad right now!"

Win looks incredulous. "Mate, if Crowky's got your grandad—and I'm almost certain he has—then feathers are *not* the issue. Crowky's probably stuffed him by now!"

"Stuffed him?" The words have a familiar ring to them. "Win . . . what do you mean?"

"You know, *stuffed*, what Crowky does when he catches someone—first he squeezes them and drains all the life out of them, and if he clings on for long enough they turn into a scarecrow."

I nod and a horrible memory comes back to me of Crowky wrapping his arms around me and refusing to let go, and how I felt weaker and weaker and weaker, until Rose leaped on his back and I managed to escape. But Grandad wouldn't have had anyone to leap on his back. . . . "Win, if Crowky drains you completely and stuffs you, you can get better, right?"

Win nods. "Mitch told me that the touch of a friend can bring you back, if they can get to you in time. I've never actually seen it happen, but Mitch is usually right about stuff."

"And if a friend doesn't get to you in time?"

Win shrugs. "You're a scarecrow for life."

Right now I feel so weak I can barely push the net away from my face. Draining . . . stuffing . . . these are all things Rose and I would have made up in a game, for fun, to drive each other mad, and Crowky's gone and done it to Grandad. "Please, Win," I say. "You've got to get me out of here."

"Don't worry, Arthur." He reaches behind his back and unsheathes a lethal-looking sword. "Me and my wakizashi have got this covered." Then he pulls back his arm, preparing to strike.

I eye the glittering blade. "That doesn't look like it's made out of a ruler."

"Nah, mate." Win narrows his eyes and takes aim. "My wakizashi is a step up from my bokken. It's made from triple-folded nymph steel. It can cut through granite . . . and bone." Then he swings the sword through the air and slices through the rope.

This time I hit the pool like a cannonball because a surprisingly heavy boy—half wizard, half ninja—is sitting on my head. And the water doesn't just go up my nose, it also goes into my eyeballs and enters my brain . . . I think . . . because suddenly . . . everything has gone . . . very . . . very . . . cold . . . and . . . black.

CHAPTER 15

I come around in a shadowy place that smells of bonfires and popcorn.

I'm slumped on a beanbag and Win is sitting next to me playing a one-man game of Hungry Hungry Hippos. For a moment I just stare as Win's hands fly around and the hippos gobble up little white balls. I squeeze my eyes shut, then open them again. Win's hands are still flying around and the hippos are still gobbling.

If crawling through the cot and into Roar was a dream, then I should have woken up back in the attic. But I'm not in the attic. I'm in a cave that's messy with dropped clothes and abandoned toys and comics. Ninja robes hang from a jutting rock and a strange collection of weapons are stashed in a leather trunk.

Win sees that my eyes are open and immediately leans over and starts thumping my chest. "*Breathe*, Arthur, *breathe!*"

"I can't . . . you're . . . punching . . . me."

"Oh, sorry. I thought you might be dead."

I'm too dazed to ask why he was playing Hungry Hungry Hippos if he thought I was dead. Instead I let my eyes wander around the cave, taking in Win's hammock, his shoebox of apples, and the glow of a fire burning just outside. I vaguely remember that Win always kept a fire going there, ready for roasting marshmallows or making toast.

My memories of Win's cave become more solid until I'm sure that if I turn my head I will see a stash of firewood and a cauldron sitting high on a shelf. I look to the left, and there they are, a pyramid of logs and a rusty cauldron, just where I knew they would be.

One thing I know for certain: I've been here before.

Win gives me a shake. "Hey, Arthur, you've only been back an hour and look how much fun we're having. First, you got trapped in that net—"

"By you."

"Right. Then you fell in that pool and nearly drowned!"

"Because of you."

"You're welcome. And now I've saved your life!" He throws his arms around me and gives me a big hug. "It's so good to have you back, Arthur." He squeezes me tight. "Roar needs its masters, and seeing as Rose isn't here we'll have to make do with you."

I open my mouth to complain about this, but already Win's dropped me back on the beanbag and jumped to

his feet. He darts around the cave practicing ninja moves. "Leaping tiger kick!" he shouts, knocking over a pile of comics. "Iron fist punch!" He spins around and delivers a deadly blow to a pillow. Then he whips out his wand and moves on to spells. "Belly wham!" he cries, and the pillow bursts open in an explosion of feathers and blue smoke. "Cheese storm!" Green stars shoot from Win's wand and the comics flutter up into the air, then scatter across the floor.

"Oh . . ." Win takes in his trashed cave. "I was trying to tidy up."

"Still working on the magic?" I say.

He frowns at his wand. "Yep."

Just then I spot Grandad's asthma inhaler poking out of his pocket and my head clears enough to remember why I'm here. I stagger to my feet, reach out, and grab the inhaler from Win. "I've got to get to Grandad," I say, but before I've taken a step my legs buckle under me and I crash back down.

Win throws me an apple. "Eat this. It

will build up your energy." Obediently I bite into the apple. It's sweet and tastes of butterscotch jelly beans—nothing like normal apples—and after a few bites I'm able to stand up. Clinging to the bumpy wall, I make my way toward the entrance of the cave, determined to find Grandad.

Win trots along by my side. "Were you surprised when you saw me in the attic, Arthur?"

"Very," I say, pausing while a wave of dizziness washes over me. "How did you do it?"

"I'm not sure, but I reckon it had something to do with this." He reaches inside his robes and pulls out a golden chain. Hanging from the chain is a lime-green fidget spinner. "Behold: the Relic of Arthur!" He touches it with a finger, making it spin. "Isn't it beautiful?"

I stare at the fidget spinner, which I'm fairly certain I found in a bin at the park. "I don't know if I'd call it *beautiful . . .*"

"You're right. It's miraculous because I've been visiting that tunnel for months, trying to get to Home, and the first time I wore this it took me straight to you. Can you imagine what would happen if Crowky got hold of it? He'd be visiting Home every day!"

Win's words are enough to get me moving again. At the mouth of the cave I see a network of paths leading off into a forest.

I don't bother asking Win which way to go; he was always getting us lost. Instead I reach for the map, and that's when I remember it flying out of my hands by the waterfall. I groan.

"What's up?" says Win.

"I had this map of Roar, but I lost it!"

Win's eyes light up and he pulls out his wand. "Salty grin!" he cries, and thick yellow smoke fills the air.

I cough and squeeze my eyes shut, and when I open them again Win is holding the map in his hands.

I laugh in amazement. "Win . . . that was *really* good magic!"

He shrugs. "Actually the map was in my pocket. I found it by the pool when I pulled you out."

"So . . . why did you do the spell?"

He grins sheepishly. "Just wanted to know what it felt like to do an awesome spell."

I'm not sure Win understands just how urgent this situation is, but at least I've got the map and can get my head around where I've got to go. I open it and find the Crow's Nest. The castle is stuck out at sea surrounded by huge waves. I have no memory of being inside it, and suddenly I realize why. "We never got there, did we?"

Win shakes his head. "We tried, but the sea there is so wild that only the *Raven* can reach the Crow's Nest. Any other boat would be smashed to pieces."

I stare at the crooked towers on the castle. At Crowky's grinning face. "Win, if that's where Grandad's been taken, then I've got to get in there!"

"It's OK. I know a secret way. It's the scarecrow army you should be worrying about. Crowky's got loads of them guarding the Crow's Nest."

"The scarecrow army . . . what's that?"

"What do you think? An army of scarecrows! Crowky started making them after you left. They're like violent scarecrow zombies and I reckon Crowky controls them with his *mind*."

I stuff the map into my pocket and stagger toward the trees. "Win, don't say another word. Let's just go and get Grandad before anything bad happens to him."

I'm about to step into the forest when Win yells, "Surprise hand grab!" and yanks me back. He looks nervous. "We can't go now, Arthur. It's almost nighttime."

"But you're half ninja. I thought ninjas loved creeping around in the dark."

"Darkness *is* my friend and I can melt into it, but it's also when the scarecrow army goes on the rampage. In fact"—his eyes flick out into the gloomy forest and he drops his voice to a whisper—"they're probably out there right now, *listening* to us! It's at night that they cause most of their mayhem."

"What sort of mayhem? Do they go around breaking stuff?"

Win shakes his head violently. "No! They go around *eating* stuff."

And that's when a twig snaps somewhere in the trees.

I shuffle closer to Win. "Did you hear that? It was

probably a rabbit, right? There were always loads of rabbits in Roar."

"Not since the scarecrows started catching them to make into hats."

"*What?*"

"I keep trying to tell you, Arthur, a lot has changed in Roar." He takes a step back from the forest. "There's one more thing you should know about Crowky's scarecrow army. . . ."

"What's that?"

"They're excellent at standing still."

The dark forest stretches out in front of us. "What, like standing still between trees?"

"*Especially* between trees."

Suddenly Win lets go of me, takes a step forward, and cries out, "Arthur Trout, Master of Roar, is back, you bunch of *dingly-dangly idiots*, and he's going to rip your straw-stuffed heads from your bodies and shove them where the sun don't shine, so COME AND GET IT!"

"*LATER!*" I shout. "I'll do all that later!"

But already something is stepping out of the trees, something that is big and dark and has spectacularly sparkly teeth.

CHAPTER 16

I gasp, my heart pounding. "*Orion?*"

The mighty stallion stalks toward me. He has nostrils like buckets and his muscles are gigantic and rippling. He looks absolutely nothing like the rocking horse in the attic.

He stomps around, trampling through the glowing coals of the fire and lowering his head to peer into the cave. He seems to be looking for something. Suddenly he turns and clip-clops his way back to me, only it's more *CLIP! CLOP! CLIP!* and sparks explode where his hooves strike the ground.

"Er . . . I might make us some toast," says Win, edging away.

"Win, don't go. Orion hates me!"

"Not as much as he hates me," he says, and he slips into the cave.

Orion stares at me and tosses his mane.

"Really?" I dare to look him in the eye. "You hate Win more than you hate me?" Somehow, by raising his shoulders and narrowing his eyes, Orion manages to imply *only just*. Then he steps toward me, forcing me backward until I'm pushed up against the rock face. He lifts up one hoof and presses it into my chest.

"What's the matter, Orion? Are you angry with me? I was never *really* going to throw you out of the attic window. . . . Or are you annoyed because Rose isn't here?"

His big head rises, then falls. He's nodding.

"You are? Well, don't blame me! Rose could have come, but she chose to go to Claire's instead!" I'm gibbering now, but I can't help it. I get the feeling that if Orion wanted to, he could push his hoof straight through me like a skewer in a kebab. He bares his dazzling teeth. "What do you want?!" I cry.

He steps back and starts pawing the ground and tossing his mane from side to side. He rears up until he's towering over me, then crashes back down. His tail whips around and a few strands of hair catch my arm. Pain shoots through me. It's like thousands of needles jabbing into me . . . or being stung by bees.

As I clutch my arm I realize that Rose made this happen. Orion's tail never used to sting, but just by saying some words in the attic yesterday, Rose changed something in Roar.

Win edges out of the cave. "Arthur, what've you done to him? Why's he so angry?"

"I've not done anything! He wants Rose."

I look into Orion's wild eyes. "She's not in Roar. She's at home, where we come from, and she might be freaking out a bit right now, but she's totally safe, trust me." Orion thinks for a moment—I know he's thinking because his glittery eyeballs have become narrow slits—then he nods, showing he's accepted what I've said. After one last glower he turns to leave.

"Don't go." I run forward. "Our grandad is in Roar and Crowky's got him at the Crow's Nest. Can you help us get there? Give us a lift or something?"

Orion flashes me a disgusted look, then rears up on his

hind legs and leaps into the forest.

"That horse has got melting into darkness *nailed*," says Win as Orion and his thundering hooves vanish into the night. "Don't worry, mate. Tomorrow, when the scarecrow army is nice and quiet, we'll find your grandad and get him back. We don't need that great big horse to help us."

I'm not just worried; I'm scared too. I don't remember feeling like this when we used to play Roar. If we felt fear, it was the exciting, fun type, like when you go on a roller coaster or listen to a ghost story. I put my hand to my chest. It aches from where Orion pressed his hoof into me and I can feel my heart thudding. There is nothing fun about what I'm feeling right now. "We can do this, can't we, Win?" I look at him for reassurance. "We can go to the Crow's Nest, get past Crowky, and save my grandad?"

I'm expecting Win to say, "Course we can!" but for a moment he just stands there thinking.

"I wasn't joking when I said Crowky had changed," he says. "He was always mean, but now he's vicious, and with his army he's powerful too. It feels like he's everywhere." Win's eyes flick back to the forest. "He used to have a few scarecrows working for him—things that got stuffed and stayed stuffed, a couple of unicorns, a mermaid—but now that he's made his army I'm always waiting, wondering what he's going to do next. He's taking over Roar." He looks at me and grins. "But now you're back, Arthur, and I know you can sort Crowky out, just like you used to!"

Win isn't making me feel any better. In fact, I feel sick with worry. "We need Rose. She always came up with our plans to get Crowky, and she was never scared of him." *Unlike me.*

"Well, Rose isn't here, but we have got you." He pulls my arm. "Come on. I want to show you something."

We go along a path that skirts the edge of the forest. All the time Win keeps glancing into the trees, pausing every few steps to listen. Soon we come to a cave and Win lights a candle. He passes it to me and whispers, "Go on. See what's inside."

Holding the flickering candle up high, I walk deeper into the cave, then I stop and look around.

At first I don't understand what I'm seeing. The cave is full of objects arranged on rocky shelves. I step closer. A butterfly hair clip sits next to an empty chip bag. A scrap of paper with a game of hangman drawn on it is arranged on a ledge next to a single rain boot with a hat propped on top. A Batman key ring (missing one leg) dangles from a nail, and at the back of the cave I find a carefully folded T-shirt and a metal pot of green putty.

The putty is set on its own ledge with an upturned plastic cup acting as a stand. "After the Relic of Arthur, *that's* my favorite thing," whispers Win. "You left it behind four years ago, just after your birthday."

And that's when I realize that this cave is a museum full of things that once belonged to me and Rose. I turn in a circle and the candle lights up curling stickers and animal erasers, a lone gummy bear, a book without a cover and a whole collection of candy wrappers threaded on a piece of string. "Where did all this come from?"

"All over Roar," says Win proudly. "I found most of it, but the unicorns brought things too. And look!" He points to the wall and I lift the candle higher. Hoof prints cover the soft, sandy walls, hundreds of them, overlapping each other. Above the hoof prints, someone—Win, I'm guessing—has carved "ROSE AND ARTHUR, MASTERS OF ROAR."

"I made this when you didn't come back. To begin with it was just for me, and to keep your things safe, but when things got bad the unicorns started to visit, and then the fuzzies. It made us feel better . . . safer."

I pick up a Pokémon trading card. "Why did you want to show me this, Win?"

"You need to know that you're a Master of Roar, Arthur, just like Rose, and if anyone can defeat Crowky, it's you."

I swallow, and put the Pokémon card back on its shelf. "You reckon?"

"Absolutely. Now let's go and sit by the fire, make some toast, and come up with a super-stealthy plan to get your grandad back!"

CHAPTER 17

The next morning, after a quick breakfast of more toast and apples, Win and I stand outside the cave, ready to set off for the Crow's Nest.

The cool air wakes me up, which is good because I didn't sleep well. All night I lay on the floor of the cave, tossing and turning in my sleeping bag and worrying about Grandad. I worried about Rose too. When she got back from town and realized I was gone she would have been scared. But I kept reminding myself that she could have come with me if she wanted to. In fact, she could be standing next to me right now as Win runs through the mission briefing.

"Weapons?" says Win, making sure his wakizashi is strapped to his back.

"Check," I say. Win's lent me a rucksack and I've put the most effective wooden sword I could find in it. I'd have taken his bokken too, but right now it's lying at the bottom of the On-Off Waterfall.

"Emergency supplies?" says Win.

"Check." Stuffed on top of the swords are a handful of apples.

"First-aid kit?"

"Check." I pat my pocket, which contains bandages. I can also feel the map in there and that's reassuring, like there's some order to this strange world I've found myself in.

Win fixes me with a look. "Relay the mission logistics, Arthur."

"Pardon?"

He rolls his eyes. "Tell me what we're going to do."

"Oh, right. We're going to go to the Crow's Nest, fight Crowky, then rescue my grandad." I try to make my voice sound confident. I badly want to believe that in a few hours' time I'll be bundling Grandad back into the tunnel and taking him home. But then, as I picture where we're about to go—to a castle that sits on a rock, far out at sea—I remember the massive flaw in our plan. "Win, exactly *how* are we going to get to the Crow's Nest?"

Win's eyes widen. "Let's just say I've got a little surprise for you. . . ."

I slip my hand into my pocket and wrap it around Grandad's inhaler. "I'm really not up for any surprises right now, Win."

"OK, OK . . . we're going to get to the Crow's Nest by going along *the Magic Road!*"

"What magic road? I don't remember any magic road in Roar."

"That's because it's new. It appeared a couple of weeks ago."

"Like magic?" I suggest.

"Exactly!"

"So the only hope we've got of rescuing my grandad is if we use a magic road?"

"Not any old magic road," says Win. "*The* Magic Road!" Then he yanks down his ninja hood, cries, "This mission is GO!," jumps on the nearest bike—the one that has

functioning brakes, I notice—screams, and pedals into the forest. I have no choice but to pick up the other bike and follow him. I scream too. Only my scream isn't a war cry, it's one of terror because I'm cycling through a forest on a bike without brakes.

"Watch out for the crack!" Win calls over his shoulder.

"What crack?" I shout. Then I spot a jagged line cutting across the path in front of me and shoot straight over it.

Win laughs. "That crack!"

CHAPTER 18

Despite all my worries, it's impossible not to enjoy our bike ride through Roar. I'm with Win, the sun is shining, and it's hard to feel stressed when you're on a bike. Plus I keep seeing incredible things that I'd forgotten existed, like monkeys that sleep in trees in tangled balls and long lines of spotted beetles and snails that hum as they move.

Every now and then we pass another crack in the ground, just like the one I cycled over. I catch up with Win and ask him where they've come from.

"It's actually just one crack," he says. "It cuts right across Roar, from my cave to the Bottomless Ocean."

Before I can ask what he's talking about, he yells, "PEDAL POWER!" and zooms ahead, weaving through an orchard of apple trees. I follow, my wheels crunching over apples and filling the air with the smell of butterscotch.

As we're coming out of the orchard I spot my first fuzzy. It's swinging on a branch like a hamster dangling from the bars of its cage. "Fuzzy!" I shout. Its bulgy eyes fix on me and it drops from the branch and starts flying around my face, making a high-pitched whining sound. I have to stop pedaling—I can't see a thing—and that's when I realize the fuzzy is talking to me.

"ArthurArthurArthur!" it's saying over and over again. Then it wraps its tiny arms around my neck, gives me a furry squeeze, and zigzags off through the trees.

"Come on," calls Win, "or we'll miss the Magic Road!"

We cycle through a valley, then cut across a meadow filled with enormous sunflowers. I'm so busy looking up at them that I almost crash into the back of Win. I slam my feet down and skid to a halt.

"Why've you stopped?" I say, but when I look over his shoulder I understand.

Directly in front of us is a dark, gaping sinkhole. It's so big Grandad's house could disappear inside it. Win gets down on his hands and knees and peers over the edge. "You've got to look, Arthur. . . . It's the weirdest thing."

Cautiously I kneel next to him. Roots and stones stick out of the sinkhole's crumbling sides, and there's even a tree caught upside down between two rocks. I can't see the bottom of the hole, just pitch-black nothing. I start to feel dizzy. I hate the idea of falling, and falling into this thing would be terrifying.

"When did it appear?" I say.

"About a year after you left. I saw it happen. One minute

there was a hill here, covered in trees and flowers and birds, and the next—BOOM!—everything was gone. Well, the birds were still there, hovering around in the dust and looking confused."

I stare into the darkness. "It looks deep."

"Yeah, I reckon it's bottomless." To prove his point Win picks up a rock and throws it into the hole. We don't hear it land. We just kneel there, listening, as cold, damp air washes over us. After a moment Win adds, "I think Crowky might chuck stuff down there."

Immediately I picture Grandad tumbling into the blackness. "What makes you say that?"

Win shrugs, then gets to his feet. "Like I said, things have disappeared—the unicorns, some merfolk—and they started disappearing when these holes showed up."

I shiver. The sun is shining, but the chill of the sinkhole seems to have crept inside me. "Let's get out of here," I say, picking up my bike.

Keeping well away from the edge, we circle the sinkhole, then cut across a field. It's only when I'm pedaling hard, freewheeling through grass filled with yellow butterflies, that I manage to shake off the sinister feeling left by the sinkhole. *Rose*, I think as one of the butterflies sits on my hand before flying away. Rose has always loved yellow.

But as we cycle farther across Roar the sunshine and butterflies disappear. The trees become taller and lose their leaves, grass is replaced by dust, and clouds roll over the sun.

After a while I realize I haven't seen or heard a bird in ages. Except crows. They sit in the trees, watching us as we go past, cawing to each other.

We stop for a rest at the edge of a forest. "Well, we're definitely in the Bad Side," I say.

Win nods and we take in the twisted limbs of trees and the spiders scurrying through dry leaves. The Bad Side was always full of things Rose and I were scared of. Which is why right now fluffy cats slink between the trees and silvery spiderwebs cover the ground like a thick mat. The cats stare at us. Their eyes shine in the gloom.

"I don't like it," I say.

"Neither do I." Win glances around uneasily. "We're in Crowky territory here. We'd better put on some camouflage." He pulls a couple of purple and yellow felt-tip pens from his pocket and starts scribbling on his cheeks. "The first rule of being a ninja is to blend into your background."

He hands me the pens and to keep him happy I draw a couple of lines on my forehead. "Win, our faces are purple and yellow. What background do you think we're going to blend into?"

"A stormy desert."

"But the Crow's Nest is in the middle of the sea."

"Ah!" Win holds up a finger. "The second rule of being a ninja is, be prepared for any eventuality."

"Like the eventuality of the sea turning into a desert overnight?"

"*Exactly.*" Suddenly Win's smile disappears and he grabs my arm. "Arthur, can you hear that?"

At first all I can hear is a whining meow of a particularly fluffy white cat, but then I pick up on another sound, the distant thud, thud, thud of tramping feet. "What is it?"

Win's eyes are round with panic. "*The scarecrow army! We've got to hide!*" He shoves his bike into the cobwebs and starts to climb the nearest tree. The bare branches are draped in more cobwebs and Win squeezes himself inside them. I go to follow him, but he pushes me back with his foot. "Find your own tree, Arthur. This one's mine!"

The marching footsteps get louder, and in a blind panic I run from tree to tree, but I can't find any with a branch low enough for me to climb up.

"Hide, Arthur!" Win hisses.

Between the trees I see movement—shadowy figures— and I throw myself facedown on the ground and lie as still as possible. A fat tabby cat comes and sits next to me and flicks its tail in my face. Its deep purr vibrates through me. It was Rose who didn't like fluffy cats after one bit her when we were playing in the alleyway behind our house. But the spiders were my thing. *Still are my thing*, I think, as I'm forced to bury my face into their sticky webs.

The marching feet come to a stop. I raise my head a fraction and see four scarecrows standing shoulder to shoulder staring into the trees. I freeze as their button eyes flick left and then right. They're wearing a jumble of ragged clothes, and straw pokes out of their loose seams. Their mouths are grim stitched lines.

I shut my eyes and try to breathe as quietly as possible. Something small with lots of legs scurries over my cheek.

Seconds, then minutes tick by. The cat sniffs my face. Then I hear Win drop down from the tree. Next thing I know he's pulling me to my feet. He grins and his felt-tipped scribbles stretch across his face. "Good job we had our camouflage on!" he says, brushing a spider off my shoulder.

"Thanks for not letting me into your tree," I mutter. "They nearly saw me!"

"*Never* share your tree, Arthur. That's the third rule of being a ninja."

I shake my head as I reach for my bike. Then I see something that makes cold shock slam through my body. "Win," I whisper, "*They're still here!*"

The four scarecrows are standing at the edge of the forest. They have their backs to us and their arms are outstretched. I'm trying to decide if I should throw myself back down in the leaves or make a run for it when Win starts laughing. "They're not *really* here," he says.

"What do you mean?"

"Come and see." Before I can stop him he walks toward the scarecrows. He doesn't sneak from tree to tree or keep low to the ground. He just strides straight up to them bold as anything.

I run to catch up with him. "Are you sure this is safe?"

"*Yes*, look." He pulls me around in front of the scarecrows.
It's a chilling sight. They sway over us, their mismatched
button eyes staring into the distance, their tangled straw
hair blowing in the wind. Win stands close to one wearing a
battered top hat. He waves his hand in front of its sack face.
"Hello?" he says. "Anybody in there?" He turns to me and
grins. "See? No one's at home."

I step up to a scarecrow wearing a ragged robe. Tattered

sleeves billow around stiff arms and stick fingers point to the sky.

"So *right now* this is just a scarecrow?" I say, amazed by how still the scarecrow is. "How does Crowky control them?"

Win shrugs. "If he's near them, he talks to them—it's all caws and clicks—but I don't know how he does it when he isn't around. Remember Crowky is half crow, and crows communicate in strange ways."

And they are clever, I think as I study the scarecrows in front of me. Somehow Crowky worked out how to make these things *and* bring them to life.

Automatically I look at the scarecrow's button eyes. Suddenly they seem less dull. I might be imagining it, but have they narrowed slightly? I hear a tiny scraping sound and my eyes shoot toward the scarecrow's stick fingers. They're not outstretched anymore, but curled at the tips, as if they're about to ball into fists.

"Probably the wind did that. . . ." says Win.

"Probably."

Win's eyes slide toward me. "Shall we crack on?"

"Yep," I say, then the two of us start walking toward the forest. Without warning a group of crows burst from a tree and rise up in the air. I didn't even realize they were sitting there.

Win and I speed up, breaking into a run the second our feet hit the dead leaves. We grab our bikes, jump on, and start pedaling. Spiders skitter out of our way and cats dash in front of our path, but we don't slow down.

The rasping cry of the crows follows us as we hurtle through the forest, desperate to get as far away from those button eyes as possible.

CHAPTER 19

We stay in the shadows of the forest until we reach a path that winds up into the mountains. We climb higher and higher until there isn't a bird or blade of grass in sight, just stones and rocks and volcanic dust that gets into my eyes and throat. When I feel like my lungs might burst I stop to catch my breath and check the map.

There's not far to go. The Crow's Nest is just ahead of us, beyond the next mountain, where the cliffs meet the sea. I push off and pedal hard after Win, trying to ignore the pain in my legs. Seeing those scarecrows has frightened me. Is that what Grandad is like right now? Cold and trapped and staring into space?

Up ahead Win disappears around a bend and I follow. "Win!" I shout. "When you get stuffed, how long have you got?"

"Before you turn into a scarecrow for good? We never knew for sure, but Rose said it was to do with how old you were. You're eleven, so you'd have eleven hours."

I almost smile. That's just the sort of bizarre rule Rose or I would have made up, but if Win is right, at least that gives us seventy-two hours to get to Grandad. . . . No, less than that by now. The thought makes me pedal with a renewed energy, forcing my way up the hill.

When my heart is racing and I don't think I can go any farther, the path levels out and we start to go downhill.

"Look, there's the crack," says Win.

The crack in the earth now runs alongside the path. Mist rolls down from the mountaintop, and we follow the crack as it leads toward the sound of thundering waves. When I can taste the salty tang of the sea, I know we're getting close. Win hits the brakes and I skid to a stop behind him. "We're here!" he shouts.

We've come out on a rocky cliff. Mist swirls around us and the wind is so powerful I have to hold on tight to the handlebars of my bike. The Bottomless Ocean lies in front of us, its waves pounding at the base of the cliff. The mist thins and, far across the sea, I see a monstrous shape rising out of the water.

"The Crow's Nest," I whisper.

Win puts a hand on my shoulder. "We're nearly there, mate."

Crowky's castle clings to a rock and looks impossibly tall. It has four towers that twist like blackened branches toward the sky, and each tower is topped by a jumble of twigs that look like giant rooks' nests. Round windows puncture the walls, light flickering behind them. Even though the sea separates us, I still feel like the windows are blinking eyes, watching me.

I swallow. "It's a bit . . . bigger than I remember. . . ." Suddenly, more than anything, I wish that Rose was standing next to me. I could do with some of her fearlessness right now. "So where's this Magic Road?"

Win sits down and points at the sea. "Keep watching and you'll see it. It's magic, remember?"

I sit next to him. "Yeah, you keep saying."

"Magic," Win whispers, "like me!" Then he points his wand, cries, "Plump bubble!," and a small balloon appears in the air. It deflates with a sad squeal, disappearing over the edge of the cliff. He turns to me with an awestruck look. "I've never magicked up a balloon before!"

"I liked it," I say, then we go back to staring at the sea.

The Bottomless Ocean is wild here. Waves smash against each other and the wind flies over the surface of the sea with a mournful wail. I can see the jagged mountain peaks of the End far away in the distance. Sitting here with Win, I feel like I'm at the very edge of the world. No. I feel like I'm at the very edge of something far stranger than the world. This is a good feeling because it makes me think anything could happen now . . . a Magic Road could even appear that will lead us all the way to the Crow's Nest.

Only it doesn't appear, and after half an hour all that's happened is Win's done some more rubbish magic and I've got an achy bum. "It's just waves, Win," I say. "Loads and loads of waves."

"Look . . . !" He scrambles forward and points. "There it is: the Magic Road!"

All I can see is the sea, same as before, but then a wave sucks back and I spot something just under the surface. It's a big flat rock covered in seaweed. And then I see another and another, until the waves roll over them and they disappear.

"They'll come back," says Win.

He's right. Slowly the tide goes out, making the sea level drop until a whole line of rocks is revealed. The rocks stretch all the way to the Crow's Nest.

"I found it the day after the ground cracked open," says Win. "This is where the crack runs out across the sea and somehow it pushed the land up, although you can only see it at low tide." He nudges me and grins. "If we follow it, we can stroll up

to the Crow's Nest and walk right in!"

I look at the chain of rocks. They do lead to the Crow's Nest, but it's not like any road I've ever seen. A road is smooth and covered in asphalt, and you can travel along it safely. But these rocks have great big gaps between them—like giants' stepping stones—and in some places the road is just a pile of boulders covered in seaweed. I squint into the distance. "You really think we can go along there and get to the Crow's Nest?"

Win nods confidently. "I know we can. I've done it!"

"Really? You climbed over all those rocks, jumped over the gaps, and got to the castle before the tide came in?"

"Well, not *all the way*," Win admits, "but close. It was getting dark and I was hungry and I saw this massive octopus." He shivers. "It *really* freaked me out . . . but I'm sure I could have done it if I'd wanted to."

I lean forward. The road starts about halfway down the cliff. "How did you even get onto the first rock?"

Win's eyes light up. "That's the best bit: to get to the Magic Road we have to go down the Magic Tunnel!"

Of course we do. Before I can even ask what the Magic Tunnel is, Win's jumped up and climbed on his bike. "Come on," he says.

I cycle after Win back the way we've just come. After a few minutes he stops and points at the ground. "Look." The crack disappears into the rock face at this point, but when Win lifts a curtain of shriveled ivy I realize that it's actually cut a narrow tunnel right through the rock.

"Behold the Magic Tunnel," Win says, then he pushes off and cycles between the leaves.

I follow him down the dripping tunnel, the wheels on my bike slithering over wet stones. Win starts whooping as our bikes shoot along, getting faster and faster.

"What's so magical about this tunnel?" I shout, ducking to avoid a dangling root.

"It's so steep!" Win cries, and I see that he's right. The tunnel is sloping dramatically downhill. I squeeze my brakes. Then I remember that I don't have any brakes.

My bike picks up speed. "Win . . . where does this tunnel come out?"

"Here!" he cries, hitting his brakes. "Right on the Magic Road!" I swerve to the left and zoom past him. Directly ahead is the opening of the tunnel. "Mate!" Win calls. "You might want to slow down!"

I put my feet on the ground, but all this does is make tiny stones fly up in my face. "I CAN'T!" I yell, and my bike hurtles out of the tunnel, straight toward a thin spit of rock covered in seaweed. I see the flash of waves smashing against it as I shoot straight across it

"Keep pedaling!" yells Win. "And don't look down!"

I do what he says. I don't have any choice. I zoom along the spit of rock until it opens out into a lovely wide space. Suddenly the wheels of my bike skid on a fat bit of seaweed, the bike slips out from under me, and I crash to the ground. Sea spray rains down and the wheels on the bike spin.

Win laughs. "SO GNARLY!"

I lift up my head and see him standing at the mouth of the tunnel. After carefully propping his bike up, he picks his way over the narrow rock, avoiding the worst bits of seaweed and pausing whenever a particularly large wave strikes.

He helps me to my feet. "That was the most awesome thing I've ever seen in my life. I was tempted to try it myself, but, you know . . ."

"You didn't want to die?" I pull seaweed out of my hair

and shuffle toward the middle of the rock, where it feels a bit safer.

"Yeah, something like that."

"So what now?" I look along the line of rocks that leads to the Crow's Nest. From down here the castle manages to appear both enormous and unnervingly far away. Mist drifts across the sea and starts to roll over the Magic Road.

"We start jumping," says Win. "It's fun."

He walks to the edge of the rock we're standing on and takes a big leap, landing on the next one.

I go to follow him, but when I get to the edge, I stop. The rock I'm standing on is big and flat. It feels safe, but the next rock is about a meter away and it's small and curved. Win made it look easy, just jumping across like that, but now my toes are hovering on the edge I'm not sure if I can make it. And when the waves pull back I see the drop.

Win shouts back, "Do you want to save your grandad, Arthur?" and then he's off, leaping from one rock to the next.

So I focus on Grandad trapped somewhere inside that castle, arms outstretched, cold and alone, and I jump across the gap. I land clumsily, my knees slamming down and my hands scraping across barnacles, then I get to my feet. One down, only another fifty or so to go. "I'm coming!" I shout.

CHAPTER 20

We don't just get to jump over rocks, we also have to climb a small cliff, inch our way along a rock so narrow it's like walking a tightrope (a tightrope covered in seaweed), and scramble through a tunnel dripping with seawater. But still the Crow's Nest doesn't seem to be getting any closer.

Once, when Rose and I were staying with Grandad, we swam out to a diving platform in the sea. From the beach it looked easy, but I soon got tired and only managed to reach the platform because Rose kept me calm. There's no Rose to keep me calm now. Just Win, a wizard-ninja who keeps shouting, "MAGIC!" at the top of his voice and laughing like a maniac whenever a big wave hits us.

Win also does a lot of reminiscing, and seems keen to focus on all the terrible things we've done to Crowky. "Do you remember when Rose stole his head?" he calls as he walks along a rock, his arms out for balance. "She put it on a unicorn's horn and the unicorn ran into the forest and

Crowky went dashing after it, bumping into trees and falling over. Oh, and then there was that time we nicked the *Raven* because Crowky had been terrorizing the mermaids. You must remember that!"

"Kind of," I say weakly.

Now the mist is so thick I can only see the rock that's directly in front of me. The Crow's Nest is completely hidden from view. This doesn't slow Win down. If anything, he starts to jump between the rocks even faster. "We tied Crowky to the mast," he shouts. "Remember? It was so funny. A bird stole some of his straw to make a nest and the mermaids came to jeer!"

Win cackles, but I don't. We pause on a rock high above the sea. "Win, don't you think Crowky will have a serious grudge against us?"

"Definitely!"

"But when we get to the Crow's Nest you're sure we can, you know, beat him, like we used to? Even without Rose?"

"Yeah . . . probably!"

"*Probably?* Win, all we've got to help us fight Crowky—a scarecrow who can drain our energy just by placing his twiggy fingers on us and squeezing—is a wooden sword and some apples!"

"Don't forget my lethal wakizashi and my even more lethal magic!"

I shake my head. "We've not thought this through properly. Rose used to come up with our best ideas. Maybe we should . . . I don't know . . . come up with a better plan?"

"A better plan than going along the Magic Road, getting into the Crow's Nest, whacking Crowky, and saving your grandad?" Win slaps me on the shoulder and the mist twists around us. "It's an AMAZING plan, Arthur, and don't forget I'm half wizard. Since you've been gone, I've learned some wicked new spells."

"Really?" This sounds promising.

"*Yes*, I can even make fruit change color. In fact, I'll get into wizard mode right now so that I'm ready." With one hand, he pulls his hood up so that it makes a pointed hat.

Suddenly the reality of what we're about to do sinks in. "Win, this thing my grandad has, asthma, it makes it hard for him to breathe. If Crowky's stuffed him, what will that do to his breathing?"

"Well, I've never been stuffed, not properly, but when Crowky drained me I felt everything sort of slow down, my breathing, my heartbeat—"

I shake my head. "Win, we can't risk mucking this up. Let's go back and find someone who can help us get in the castle, because if Crowky catches us too, there will be no one to save Grandad, or us!"

"Umm . . . Arthur?" Win is staring ahead. "I think it's too late for that."

"What do you mean?" I peer into the thinning mist. At first I can't see anything, but then I make out a black shape. It's a figure standing dead still on a rock, arms outstretched, stick fingers spread wide. It's wearing a black leather coat, ragged and torn, which swirls in the mist. Its head hangs forward and a pair of wings tremble in the wind. A solitary crow sits on its shoulder.

"Is that . . . *Crowky?*" I whisper.

"Yep," says Win, and automatically we shuffle closer together.

"He's like those scarecrows we saw earlier, right?" I stare at the top of Crowky's head. "Right now he's asleep, not *at home.*"

"Crowky's *always* at home," says Win. "Maybe he's having a rest? Or doing it to freak us out?"

In a flash, Crowky's head snaps up and a pair of round button eyes lock onto mine. Win and I grab hold of each other as Crowky's stuffed arms flop down and his wings spring open on his back. The crow takes off with a shrill *caw*, then Crowky's twig fingers curl into fists and a grin spreads across his pale sack-like face.

"Definitely doing it to freak us out," whispers Win.

In one swift movement, Crowky crouches, then springs forward and starts to jump effortlessly from rock to rock, moving closer toward us.

"Crowky's just a boy like us," I say, gripping Win's arm.

Win laughs weakly. "Not really a boy. More a scarecrow with wings."

I force myself to smile. "You're right. He's just a big straw bird!"

"With powerful legs and life-sapping hands and a deranged mind and—"

"Not helping, Win." I squeeze his arm tighter to stop my hands from shaking.

Crowky pauses in a crouch, then bounds forward again.

Win nudges me. "Don't worry, mate. He's outnumbered!"

"But I'm no good at fighting," I say, my voice a whisper, even though Crowky is still a few rocks away. "In fact, I've never properly thumped anyone in my life!"

Win snorts. "You've thumped Crowky a hundred times."

"I mean, I haven't thumped anyone outside Roar." *In real life*, I add in my head. "And I don't want to thump anyone, not even Crowky." My voice rises in panic. "At school I was a playground mediator!"

Win's eyes flick back to me. "What are you talking about, Arthur?"

"I'm trained to sort situations out using—"

"A bag of rocks? Your fists? Nunchucks?"

"No! *Words.*"

Crowky takes a flying leap and lands on the rock immediately opposite ours. His shoulders are hunched and his head is angled down again. Mist wraps around him.

"*Words*, Arthur?" says Win. "*Words? Crowky* will eat your *words*, before stuffing them back into your mouth and dumping you—and your *words*—into the sea!"

"Words are actually very powerful."

Crowky's head lifts.

"But are words as powerful as *him?*" Win hisses.

Crowky's stuffed body ripples in anticipation and his wings pull back. He stares at me and his grin spreads even wider across his moonlike face.

I'm so scared I have to remind myself to breathe.

"*Arthur Trout!*" he rasps.

I blink and try to swallow away my fear. Underneath his leather coat Crowky's wearing ripped black jeans with straw poking out of the holes and black high-tops. His dirty yellow hair sticks out as wildly as his feathers.

"When did he get so muscly?" I whisper to Win. Crowky's arms look overstuffed, bulging with straw.

"When he started eating mermaids."

"*What?!*"

He smiles weakly. "Joke."

I feel faint. "Win, do me a favor? Don't do any jokes, just for a bit."

"OK, but you need to say something. This is getting weird. . . ."

He's right. It is. Crowky is grinning at me in silence. I clear my throat and force myself to look into his hard eyes.

"Hello," I say in a small voice.

Win thumps me. "*Hello?* Say something tougher than that!"

"Um . . . Crowky, we've not come to cause you any trouble—"

"We have!" shouts Win. "Massive trouble!"

Now it's my turn to thump him. "We just want my grandad back. I don't want to blame you for something you haven't done, but all the evidence seems to point toward you having stolen him. . . ." Crowky still doesn't speak. He just watches me, his button eyes glittering. "Maybe *stolen* isn't quite the right word. I mean, maybe you were trying to *help* him? Was that it? If so, thank you for helping my grandad, but I'd like to take him home now . . . please. Perhaps we could all go back to the Crow's Nest and collect him?"

Crowky raises a hand and points a knobbly twig finger at me. "I am going to get you, Arthur Trout." His voice is a rusty-nail snarl. "I am going to get you and your sister just like I got your pathetic, sniveling grandad!"

Something hot, like fire, stirs inside me, a flicker of something that I haven't felt for a long time. I let go of Win and step forward. "My grandad has never sniveled in his life!"

The wind whips my words away and Crowky's eyes widen in delight. "Oh yes he has. He sniveled when I found him in that tunnel and pulled him into Roar, he sniveled when I chained him up in my dungeon, and he sniveled when I ripped this off his back!" He flings open his jacket to reveal that he's wearing Grandad's "NO PROB-LLAMA!" T-shirt.

I shake my head in horror. "What sort of . . . weirdo steals an old man's T-shirt?"

Crowky laughs and points at himself with both twig thumbs. "This sort of weirdo! But he still didn't shut up, Arthur, so today I was forced to drain all the moaning and sniveling out of him." As he says these words his hands press together in front of him, like he's reliving the moment he crushed the life out of Grandad.

"You stuffed my grandad?" My voice is weak.

"Oh yes, Arthur!" he says with delight. "He's a scarecrow now."

Horror crashes through me as hard as the waves hitting the rocks by my feet. Win puts his hand on my shoulder, keeping me steady.

"Where's Rose, by the way?" says Crowky, his eyes flicking behind us. "I thought I'd be catching two little Trouts today. Don't you two come as a pair?"

I lift my chin up. "Rose isn't here," I say, and I'm actually glad she didn't crawl with me into the cot. No matter what

Rose has done, I never want her to feel this scared.

Crowky smiles. "Then I'll have to make do with what I've got. Do you think your grandad would enjoy a dip in the Bottomless Ocean?" He peers down at the crashing waves. "It's difficult to swim when you can't move a muscle."

I lunge forward, but Win pulls me back, shouting, "Weapons, Arthur, weapons!"

I stick my hand into my rucksack and pull out a wooden sword. Win holds his wakizashi in one hand, and his wand in the other.

"Wait!" he whispers. "I'll hit him with a snaring spell. He won't be able to move and you can go up there and thump him." Before I can say anything Win has leaped forward, raised his wand high above his head, and cried, "Pigeon fudge!"

There's a bang, and stars and smoke burst from his wand. When the smoke clears we see that the wakizashi is now tightly gripped in Crowky's hand. With a cackle he swishes it through the air.

"I think I did the *sharing* spell by mistake," cries Win. "Did I say '*pigeon* fudge' or '*smidgen* fudge'?"

But we don't have time to discuss Win's spectacularly rubbish magic, because Crowky has raised the wakizashi high above his head and is already leaping through the air toward our rock.

"RUN!" I yell.

CHAPTER 21

We turn and run.

But we've only taken a few steps before we realize our path is blocked.

The rock behind us is now packed full of scarecrows. There are more than I can count and they are pushing and shoving at each other, apparently desperate to get at us.

"Where did they come from?" I whisper.

"The *Raven*," says Win.

Farther along the Magic Road, Crowky's battleship is tethered to a rock. It must have crept up in the mist and now it's creaking and groaning as waves smash against it. Crows circle around the sails, their caws sounding like laughter. I see more scarecrows jump from her deck, then like a swarm of scurrying creatures they rush to join the pack standing opposite us. The scarecrows stare through mismatched button eyes. Wisps of straw float off them as they hunch forward, preparing to attack. Some smile.

Some snarl. Their stick fingers twitch.

Crowky is behind us, his army is in front of us, and all around are the waves of the Bottomless Ocean. We're trapped.

"The mission hasn't quite gone according to plan," says Win as the scarecrows inch closer.

"Not quite." I hear a rustle of wings and see Crowky is closing in on us too. He's frowning in concentration, and making strange birdlike sounds—harsh caws and clicks—and, as one, the pack of scarecrows crouch into a striking position. I realize that Crowky just made them do that. Last time I was in Roar, he worked alone. Now he's commanding this army.

"Arthur?" Win shoves me. "Any bright ideas?"

My eyes flick from Crowky to the scarecrows. "Let's fight the scarecrows. There are loads of them, but if we can get past them at least we stand a chance of getting back to land. Can they stuff things, like Crowky?"

Win shakes his head. "I don't know, mate, but there's one way to find out. Ready?"

"Ready." My trembling voice gives away my fear.

Win clutches his wand in front of him. "Say that thing."

"What thing?"

"That thing you always used to shout. You know: *Hear me roar!*"

At that moment the scarecrows surge forward and I hear a great flap of wings behind me. "Hear me roar!" I yell. "HEAR ME ROAR!"

Win and I fling ourselves over the gap and onto the next rock.

The moment we hit the ground we're tugged apart. Scarecrows pull at me, scratch my face, and tear at my clothes. I stagger to my feet and try to smash my way through them. But there are too many, and they press closer and closer, punching and stamping. Then the crows join in too: pecking and jabbing, aiming for my eyes. Keeping an arm over my face, I try to fight back. I thrust the wooden sword in front of me, trying to clear a path, but it's plucked from my hands and the next thing I know it's smacking me across my shoulders. I pull a scarecrow's arm so hard that it comes off in my hands, but the scarecrow just swings around and smashes me with its other fist. Between blows I see Win struggling to hold on to his wand.

Soon the scarecrows force us together, until we're cowering at the very edge of the rock. Just when I think we're going to be shoved into the sea they fall back.

With a leap Crowky lands on our rock and strides toward us, eyes gleaming.

"Oh dear," says Win.

"*Oh dear?*" We clutch each other for support. "Win, we've been defeated in under three minutes!"

"At least we're going down in a blaze of glory!"

I see that at some point one of the scarecrows got Win's rucksack off my back and is now rummaging through it.

It pulls out one of the apples, opens its mouth, and swallows it whole.

I shake my head. "This isn't a blaze of glory. . . . It's pathetic!"

Crowky stops in front of us. "Pathetic," he says. "I couldn't have chosen a better word myself." Then in one lightning-quick movement he lunges forward and grabs hold of my shoulders. The second his twig fingers dig into my skin, a cold numbness slams into me. I try to struggle and kick out, but already my legs are becoming stiff. "*Drain . . . ,*" hisses Crowky. "*Drain . . .*"

I twist and turn, but Crowky only presses harder, his eyes rolling to the back of his head, as everything warm inside— my life, my breath—seeps away. I see Win grab Crowky's arm, but one kick sends him flying to the ground.

"Drain . . . drain." Crowky's voice is a hoarse whisper.

As the chill creeps up my neck toward my throat, Crowky seems to come to life. His head lifts, his eyes focus, and his wings start to beat, slowly at first, then faster and faster until they're a blur and then he's rising into the air.

"I'm flying!" he shrieks. "I'm FLYING!" His hands squeeze tighter and he lifts my heavy, icy body up with him.

My throat is tight, but I manage to cry, "Win, HELP!"

Win staggers to his feet and wraps his arms around my legs; instantly I feel a glow of warmth and I'm able to twist from side to side, but Crowky's grip is like steel and his wings just beat harder, pulling me higher in the air until I'm nearly being torn in two. Below me waves smash against the rocks and Crowky kicks out at Win, who's clinging onto my legs refusing to let go. Crowky pushes his face close to mine. I see a loose thread dangling from one button eye and breathe in his musty, feathery smell. "I really do have you now, don't I, Arthur Trout?" Then he throws his head back and cackles.

At that moment a screech echoes across the valley. It's followed by a thudding like distant thunder. Crowky's eyes shift from my face to the sky beyond, then his face scrunches up with rage. "NO!"

I manage to turn my head. Two vast shapes are moving through the sky, beating a path toward us.

"Dragons!" Win cries as great wings loom through the mist. There is another spine-tingling screech and a ball of fire explodes in the sky. One of the dragons leads the way, close enough now for me to see light shining through his red wings and the arrowhead tail that droops below him.

"*Pickle?*" I whisper.

A darker, larger dragon tumbles around Pickle, snapping at his tail. *Vlad.* The dragons' names come back to me as fast as they're cutting through the sky.

Pickle soars closer and closer until the flash of fire shooting from his jaws showers us with sparks. Crowky howls, and that's when I remember that if there's one thing straw-stuffed Crowky hates, it's fire.

Pickle dives and his talons stretch wide as if he's preparing to strike. Then, through the black smoke billowing from his nostrils, I see a figure sitting on his back. Her eyes are blazing and her hair is flying out behind her. She's wearing slippers and a leopard-print onesie.

"Rose!" I yell, and at that moment Crowky loses his grip and I fall backward, past the rock and toward the sea, dragging Win down with me.

CHAPTER 22

Down we go, screaming and thrashing our arms. The sea sucks back and just as we're about to smash headfirst onto the rocks, talons scrape across my back and I'm swept into the air. I see Win swinging from Pickle's other clawed hand.

Pickle's wings beat hard and we soar higher and higher, away from the Magic Road and Crowky and his army. Relief sweeps through me until I realize that as the Crow's Nest falls behind us we're leaving Grandad behind too. But when I see just how high up we are and how loosely Pickle seems to be holding me, all thoughts of anything disappear.

"My hat's burnt!" Win laughs, pulling it off his head to show me. He has a big grin on his face, but I can't even talk. I lied when I told Rose I wasn't afraid of anything. I'm afraid of loads of things, but most of all I'm afraid of heights, or rather falling. The clouds floating below my feet make my insides feel like liquid and my legs tremble.

No. It makes all of me tremble.

"Wow!" cries Win. "Look at the Tangled Forest. It's so pretty!"

"Win," I manage to say, "we're dangling in the claws of a dragon . . . about a mile off the ground. It's not pretty—it makes me want to puke." Then I squeeze my eyes shut while Win gives me a running commentary of our journey over Roar.

"I think my cave is over there. . . . Ooh, check out the tiny trees!"

I only risk a quick look down when Win tells me we're flying over the archipelago. *No, Archie Playgo*, I think, remembering the tiny islands drawn on the map. I'm tempted to try to spot more landmarks from the map, to find the Tangled Forest and the On-Off Waterfall, but I can't quite bring myself to raise my head.

Win laughs. "I haven't been here for ages. The water looks like silver!"

Floating below us are the hundreds of islands that make up the Archie Playgo. They're dotted across water that's so still I can see Pickle's and Vlad's reflections sailing below us, and even me and Win swinging from Pickle's claws. I feel myself slip ever so slightly, and shut my eyes again. If I can't see, I can almost pretend this isn't happening. But I can't ignore Pickle's deadly burps; at least I hope they're burps. Rushes of hot smelly gas keep whipping past my face, making me squeeze my mouth shut as well as my eyes. And

Vlad doesn't make the journey go any smoother. I can hear him circling us, shrieking at Pickle and trying to draw him into play fights.

"Arthur!" Win has to shout to be heard over the dragons' beating wings. "I think we're landing!"

I open one eye. He's right. We've dropped lower and are circling an island. I haven't been able to speak to Rose since Pickle snatched us to safety, but I guess she knows where she's going. As we spiral closer to the island I see it has a lagoon in the middle, and off to one side a hut with a jetty. It looks vaguely familiar and so does the dark shape meandering below the surface of the lagoon like a giant goldfish.

Pickle is gliding now, but we're not slowing down. If anything, as the ground rushes up to meet us, it feels like we're going faster.

"Do you reckon Rose has remembered we're down here?" shouts Win.

"Definitely!" I yell, but then Pickle flies so low over a field that we have to pull our legs up to stop them from being dragged along the rocky earth. "Maybe. . . ."

Moments before we smack into the ground, Pickle swings left, opens his talons, and drops us onto a pile of dry grass. For a moment we just lie there, curled up and stunned, then Win leaps to his feet and cries, "That was MIND-BLOWING! Let's do it again!"

I simply groan and savor the amazing sensation of lying

on solid ground and having a body that might be bruised, but isn't being squeezed by a scarecrow or held loosely by a dragon.

Pickle lands with a thump and Vlad crashes down next to him. Rose slides off Pickle's back and immediately the dragons start licking her face with their black tongues. Then Vlad lifts up a foot and gently knocks her to the ground, where they nuzzle her and roll her playfully about on the grass.

Rose wriggles out from underneath them and issues a stern command, making them slink away, tails curled under their bodies. As they plod over to the pool and start to drink great gulps of water, Rose stomps toward us, her slippers crunching over shells and wildflowers. She looks furious. Her normally straightened hair has sprung into curls and she's covered in grass and dragon spit.

She stops in front of me, wipes the slimy stuff off her face, and puts her hands on her hips. "*What* is going on, Arthur?"

"Rose!" Win tries and fails to give her a hug. "Thanks for saving my life. I definitely owe you one!"

Rose acts like he's invisible and continues glaring at me, so Win gives her a final squeeze, then goes off to peer into the lagoon.

"You came after me," I say.

She shrugs like it's no big deal. "When I got back from town and discovered you'd gone missing too I decided you were both playing a trick on me. So I watched some TV, then had a bath and went to bed—"

"Seriously, Rose? You watched TV, then had a bath and went to bed? Did you sleep well?"

She scowls. "No I didn't, as a matter of fact. It got later and later, and I was all on my own, and I was scared and I didn't have a clue what to do. In the morning, when you still hadn't come back, I decided to call the police. But before I did that, I crawled through the cot—even though I knew it was totally ridiculous—just to check it wasn't some weird portal to another world and—"

"You discovered it *was* some weird portal to another world?"

She frowns. "Yeah. . . . Not what I was expecting."

"And you just went through the bed, straight into the tunnel, and ended up here? It worked the first time?"

"Yep. I came out on the ledge, ducked back to miss the waterfall, then whistled for Pickle. Since then I've been flying around looking for you."

This is typical of Rose. She has to do everything better than me: running, spelling, entering fantasy worlds. She glances around, taking in the spectacular islands of the Archie Playgo.

"It's amazing, isn't it?" I say.

"I guess. . . ."

"*You guess?* Rose, it's incredible. Roar is real!"

She shakes her head stubbornly. "I don't know *what* this

place is, but it's definitely not real, is it? Not like home or school or Mum and Dad."

Under our feet the earth starts to tremble.

"Ground wobble!" shouts Win, delighted. "Don't worry. They happen all the time. You'll get used to them." After a second or two the shaking fades away.

"This place isn't safe," says Rose firmly, then she starts to walk toward the hut. "We've got to get out of here, Arthur. Go back home."

I catch up with her and grab her arm. "But we can't go home. Not until we've got Grandad."

She shakes me off. "How do you know he's even here? I'm almost one hundred percent certain that this is all some freaky dream and any second now I'm going to wake up back in the real world!"

"I know he's here because Win found this." I pull out Grandad's blue inhaler. Rose stares at the familiar L-shaped plastic tube. "And Crowky was wearing Grandad's T-shirt! We have to rescue Grandad, and if we leave now, maybe we can get back to the Crow's Nest before it's dark. Perhaps with Pickle and Vlad we'll stand a chance of beating Crowky."

Rose makes an exasperated sound. "Arthur, how can you speak like this is normal and you're planning a little trip to the Crow's Nest? *None* of this is normal." She points at Win, who is punching a sunflower. "*He* isn't normal!"

"What?" says Win. "Who's not normal?"

"No one," I say, then I lower my voice. "I'm talking like this because we've got no choice. Crowky has stuffed Grandad, Rose. Do you remember what that means? Right now Grandad is dangling somewhere in Crowky's dungeons and he can't move or talk. If Win's right, we have less than seventy-two hours to get to Grandad or he'll stay like that forever!"

Rose frowns. "That sounds like something Win made up."

"No it doesn't. It sounds like something *we* made up!" I'm almost shouting now; I have to get Rose to take this seriously.

She stares into the distance. "You're right," she says eventually. "We have to go back to the Crow's Nest and find Grandad, but we can't go now. There's nowhere to land the dragons—it's all turrets and rocks—and there are too many of those *things*."

"They're scarecrows," I say. "Crowky made them."

"Well, whatever they are, they would catch us in seconds." Win abandons his sunflower and comes over to join us. "If we're going to get into the Crow's Nest, we need help from someone with brains and good magic."

"Er, *hello*?" says Win, pointing at himself.

Rose gives him a withering look.

"Like who?" I say.

For the first time Rose smiles. "You don't know where we are, do you?"

I look around, taking in the path that circles the edge of the lagoon and the huge flat rocks. "No . . . although I feel like I've been here before."

"What if I told you that this lagoon is filled with merfolk?"

As she says this a scaly tail flips out of the water, then disappears. A moment later, a face emerges—but only the forehead and eyes—before slipping below the surface of the water again.

"And that," says Rose, nodding toward the hut, "is where Mitch lives."

Win groans. "Mitch the merwitch. She'll mock my magic. She always mocks my magic!"

"She's so sarcastic," I say. "Do we really need Mitch's help?"

"Yes!" Rose raises her chin. "You're not the only one who gets to have an imaginary friend, Arthur!"

Win tugs on my sleeve. "What's an imaginary friend?"

I look at Win's big eyes. "It's just a word me and Rose use. When we say *imaginary* what we really mean is . . . amazing."

A smile spreads across his face. "So my magic's *imaginary*! My ninja skills are *totally imaginary*! Have I got it?"

"Yep. You've got it," I say, and we follow Rose up the path to the hut.

"Mitch, you'll never guess who's back!" cries Win, hammering on the door. "You've only got both Masters of Roar on your doorstep!" When no one answers he jumps in the air, cries, "Leaping tiger kick!," and slams his foot into the door. With a loud creak it falls off its hinges and crashes to the ground.

"Mitch is *not* going to like that," says Rose.

But Win is gazing at his foot, too amazed by his own strength to consider the consequences of what he's just done. "*Imaginary!*" he whispers.

CHAPTER 23

We know something is wrong the moment we step inside.

Our feet crunch over sand, thick dust covers every surface, and the door at the back of the hut is swinging open. As we walk farther in, a yellow crab scuttles out from under a cupboard, crosses to a hole cut in the wooden floor, and drops over the side with a plop. I realize that it's fallen straight into the lagoon.

I peer into the hole. The water is clear and deep, and full of tangled weed that's dotted with fluorescent snails and tiny starfish. I have a flashback to Mitch heaving herself out of this hole—her tail hitting the planks with a wet thump—then looking at me and saying, "Oh . . . it's you."

Only there is no Mitch here now.

"Mitch?" calls Rose. "Where are you?"

There's no response. All we can hear is the sound of water lapping beneath our feet.

"I don't think she's here," I say.

Rose sticks her head into Mitch's store cupboard, then goes into her bedroom. While Win checks the deck outside, I go to investigate the fireplace. A cauldron is sitting over a long-dead fire and a cutting board lies next to it, covered with shriveled-up herbs and flowers. A knife is pressed into a moldy toadstool. It's like Mitch has walked out in the middle of making dinner . . . or a spell.

Rose runs her fingers through the dust on the bottles that line the windowsill. Bright colors start to shine through: jade, crimson, and even a pale milky liquid that's threaded with swirling silver. "Where is she?" she says.

Win comes back in. "I think she's gone."

"What? Gone out?" says Rose. "Gone hunting for ingredients?"

"No. Just . . . gone." He shrugs. "Like the unicorns and half of the merfolk. I reckon she's vanished."

Rose puts down the bottle she's holding. "What do you mean?"

"It's like I told Arthur," says Win. "Things have been disappearing. It happened around the same time the ground wobbles started and the sinkholes opened up."

"Maybe they went to the Tangled Forest," says Rose. "It's huge. Loads of things could go in there and never be seen again."

Win shakes his head. "Once I thought I saw it happen, right in front of my eyes. I was down on the beach and a mermaid was jumping over a wave. I watched her fly up in the air, and then . . . she just vanished."

Rose turns and goes over to the mantelpiece. It's covered in white shells, a horse made out of driftwood, a bracelet, and a dried-up flower. Rose stares at the shells and I see that they aren't randomly scattered like I thought. In fact, they spell out "ROSE." Rose stares and stares, then swipes her hand through the shells, sending them tinkling to the floor.

"Mermaids move fast," she says. "You know that. That one you saw, she can't have vanished. You weren't looking properly!" Rose's voice is raised. Just like me, she gets angry when she's upset. She glares at us both.

"Maybe," says Win, "but I was just over at the lagoon and I can only see *one* mermaid in there. It used to be full of them. Where've they gone?"

Rose turns and bangs out of the hut, and Win and I watch her go. She walks to the end of the deck and stands, arms folded, staring across the lagoon.

Win picks up Mitch's spell book and flicks through it. Then he says, "I think now Mitch has gone I might miss her too."

"I know what you mean." I look around the abandoned room. I may have spent more time in Win's cave than Mitch's hut, but now I'm here I can remember how this place used to be full of smoke, and the smell of herbs and spices, and the sound of Mitch's laughter. The cauldron would be bubbling and Mitch would be sitting with her tail dangling in the hole, her blue hair coiled around her.

If Win was made up of things I loved, then Mitch was made up of things Rose loved: magic, the sea, and laughing at me and Win.

"I'd better check if Rose is all right," I say, and I walk out of the hut.

Rose is standing by a hammock tied to the branches of a willow tree. She pushes the hammock with one finger.

"I'm not bothered," she says before I've said a word. "Mitch was cool, but she wasn't real. Not like my friends back home." The water in the lagoon bubbles and ripples for a moment before becoming still again.

"Perhaps you're right," I say. "Maybe she is in the Tangled Forest."

Rose shakes her head. "No . . . she loved it here."

Looking around, I can see why. It's silent and beautiful. Mitch used to get annoyed with a lot of things—especially me and Win—but there's nothing to annoy her here.

Rose turns away from me and I notice that her shoulders are shaking. I wonder if she's crying, only Rose never cries. Once a log tied to a rope swing smacked her in the face and broke her nose and she still didn't cry. . . . I did—there was so much blood.

I'm just considering putting my hand on Rose's shoulder—although I'm almost certain it will drive her mad—when I hear heavy breathing behind me. I turn and see Orion walking toward us. He's soaking wet. His glittering mane hangs in limp strands around his shoulders and water drips from his body. He must have swum between the islands of the Archie Playgo to get to Rose.

He nudges past me and dips his heavy head until it's resting against Rose's cheek. She turns, and without saying a word throws her arms around his neck and buries her face in his sopping mane.

Then they just stand there, Rose's arms squeezing tight, Orion's eyes closed, and the willow branches brushing the water.

Rose looks up at me. "We're going to go back to the Crow's Nest," she says. "We're going to get Grandad and take him home."

"You really think we can do it?"

"Of course we can." Then she grips Orion's mane and pulls herself onto his back. "I'm going to come up with a plan."

Orion jumps past me, nearly knocking me into the lagoon, then gallops off across the island with Rose clinging to his back. His thundering hooves make the dragons rise up in the sky, and I watch as they circle the island, once, twice, then soar off over the sea.

CHAPTER 24

When Rose gets back, Win and I have mended the door and started to make dinner.

Win found roots, leaves, and mushrooms in Mitch's garden and together we chopped them up and put them in the cauldron. Rose inspects the thick, murky soup. "Smells surprisingly OK," she says. Then she walks around the room, pulling open drawers and rummaging through cupboards. Eventually she rips some pages from the back of the spell book, finds a pen, and starts writing. She draws diagrams, creates lists, and covers the pages with doodles and arrows. Presumably this is her plan to get Grandad out of the Crow's Nest. I only speak to her when I take the map out of my pocket and hand it over. "This might help," I say.

"Thank you," she mutters, then I leave her to it and help Win sort Mitch's potions into two piles: Deadly Poisonous and Not Deadly Poisonous.

Dinner is almost ready when Rose tells us she needs our help. "That thing you were on. That line of rocks."

"The Magic Road," says Win.

"I think you mean the Obstacle Course of Death," I say.

Rose shakes her head with frustration and passes us the map. "Whatever. I want you to add it on here. From Pickle's back I could see that it was long, but it was broken in some places and the rocks looked like they were all different shapes and sizes. I want to know exactly where everything is, especially the big boulders."

So Win and I get to work, leaving Rose to season the soup with generous dashes of potions from the Not Deadly Poisonous pile.

I have to trust Win to do the part of the Magic Road he traveled along without me, and there's a bit at the end that is a mystery to both of us, but by the time Rose is dishing up the soup we're pretty pleased with what we've done.

We eat our strange soup sitting at the end of the jetty, our feet dangling in the lagoon. I take a sip. It might be purple and fizzing, but it tastes delicious. Maybe that's because we're so hungry. As we eat we watch the setting sun turn the water orange, then yellow, and finally a deep, dark blue. It's beautiful, but it's hard to enjoy it knowing that Grandad is trapped deep in the dungeons of the Crow's Nest.

Rose must be having similar thoughts, because suddenly she bangs down her bowl. She's wearing the bracelet that was on the mantelpiece, and the shells and sea glass catch the last of the evening light. "Right," she says, "let's talk about the plan." She clears her throat and pulls out her notes and our map. "The three of us can't get into the Crow's Nest from the Magic Road because, well, you saw what happened, so we need another way in."

"The Crow's Nest is in the middle of the wildest ocean in Roar," I say. "There is no other way in."

"Yes there is," interrupts Rose. "Remember the time Crowky fished Mitch out of the sea in a net and took her to the Crow's Nest in the *Raven?*"

"Yes!" cries Win. "She escaped by jumping from a tower."

I nod, the story coming back to me. In fact, I think we were sitting right here when Mitch told us about it.

"So there's a tunnel that leads right inside the Crow's Nest from the sea," says Rose, "and we're going to fly into it on the dragons."

"*We?*" I say. "Win and I don't fly dragons, Rose, or even sit on them. That's your job, remember? We just admire them . . . from a distance."

"Well, you're going to have to learn how to fly them because three of us, plus Grandad, will be too many to sit on one dragon. I'll fly Pickle and you two will fly Vlad. Bad Dragon is much bigger. If she was around, we could use her."

"No we couldn't," says Win. "Bad Dragon is vicious!"

"But she was never *really* bad," protests Rose. "The only

reason she was called 'Bad Dragon' was because she was so cheeky and I was always having to say stuff like, 'Spit out that fuzzy, bad dragon!'"

"Now she lives up to her name," says Win. "She's bad to the core . . . or was before she disappeared."

Rose absorbs this information, then nods. "So we forget about Bad Dragon and fly Vlad and Pickle into the cave, and while Crowky and his scarecrows are being distracted, we climb up into the castle, grab Grandad, and fly out of there."

"Hang on . . . who's distracting Crowky?" I say. "Because that is one job I would not like to have."

Rose's eyes light up. "The Lost Girls."

"*The Lost Girls?*" Win sucks in his breath. "Are you *serious?* They're savage!"

The Lost Girls are shadowy in my memory, but perhaps that's because they liked to hide. They were a gang of ferocious little girls who had a camp of tree houses deep in the Tangled Forest. They were unpredictable, and there were a lot of them. . . . I think back to how quickly Win and I were overwhelmed by the scarecrow army. "Rose is right," I say. "We need the Lost Girls. But how will we get them to the Crow's Nest? We can't fit them all on the dragons."

Rose points at the bit Win and I added to the map. "They're going to get there on the Magic Road. There are loads of them so they'll be able to fight the scarecrows and keep them away from us." She looks from me to Win.

"So it's decided? Tomorrow we go to the Tangled Forest, find the Lost Girls, and persuade them to help us. Then you two can learn how to fly a dragon."

I nod, trying to ignore the various gaping holes in Rose's plan, like the "persuade them to help us" bit, and the "you two can learn how to fly a dragon" bit.

"What could go wrong?" cries Win, and in his excitement he jumps to his feet and throws himself into the lagoon with a cry of, "Ninja bomb!" He splutters to the surface. "Water's perfect. Come in!"

Rose is adamant that she's not getting wet, so while she swings in Mitch's hammock I jump in too (only I take my jeans off first) and together we swim to the center of the lagoon.

He's right: the water is perfect.

We float on our backs and watch as the last rays of sun disappear and the stars come out.

Tomorrow I have to venture into a forest that's hiding a gang of violent little girls and learn how to ride a dragon, but right now my skin is changing from red to blue to purple as the stars shine down on me, and a mermaid is swimming around us, occasionally knocking my feet with her tail.

"I'm glad you came back, Arthur," says Win, breaking the silence.

"Me too," I reply.

CHAPTER 25

We set off for the Tangled Forest at dawn.

Rose wants us to fly there on the dragons, but Win's persuaded us to go looking for Mitch's rowboat. Apparently there's a river that runs right into the Tangled Forest, so we trudge across the island hoping Mitch's boat is still moored in its usual spot.

"I don't get why Mitch even needs a boat," I say.

Rose sighs. "She's not *just* a mermaid, Arthur. She uses it when she's collecting ingredients for spells."

"But how does she even get to it?" Mitch could move about on land, by wriggling like a seal, but she didn't like doing it and I can't imagine her regularly crossing this prickly meadow of grass and sea thistles.

"There's a tunnel that runs from the sea right into her store cupboard," says Rose, then she scowls and mutters, "Or something like that."

She's been like this since we woke up: trying hard to show she's not into Roar. When we find the crack cutting across the middle of the meadow, wider than I've seen it anywhere else, she just steps over it like she's stepping over a puddle.

"Look, Rose." I peer into the darkness. "This crack runs all over Roar!"

She rolls her eyes. "It's just a crack, Arthur."

"It came two weeks and two days ago," says Win. "I know because it was your birthday and to celebrate I'd taken some cake up to the waterfall. Just as the sun was setting there was this massive earth wobble and the crack appeared. The next day I followed it through the forest and over the dunes until it disappeared into the sea."

"Me and Arthur had a massive fight that day," says Rose, then she marches forward, calling over her shoulder, "Hurry up!"

We find Mitch's boat pulled up on a pebbly beach. From here we can see the Archie Playgo spread out in front of us, each island glowing in the early morning light. But Rose barely glances at it. Instead she grabs the front of the boat and starts heaving it toward the water. "Help me, Arthur," she snaps. "The sooner we get to the Tangled Forest, the sooner we can get Grandad and get out of here."

That's another thing she's doing: ignoring Win and acting like he isn't here.

Win doesn't seem to care. He just grabs the other end of the boat and starts pushing. Mitch's boat is a normal wooden rowboat, but with jars crammed under the seats and in every corner. Lots of them still contain ingredients Mitch collected, and as we push the boat into the water glowing ferns and wriggling blobs swish around in the jars.

The moment the boat's afloat, we jump in and Rose and I take the oars. We've barely left the island behind us when Rose starts complaining. "You've got to row faster, Arthur, or we'll never make it to the Tangled Forest!"

"You row faster!" I say, but secretly I'm wondering if she's right. We don't seem to be making much progress.

"We need a bit of help, that's all," says Win. "Give me your watch, Arthur." I hand him my Casio and he leans over the side of the boat and starts splashing it about in the water. "Come and get it!" he calls. "Arthur Trout's lovely watch!"

"Win, what are you doing? It's water-*resistant*, not waterproof!" My words die away as a dark brown hand slips out of the water. Webbed fingers snatch my watch, then disappear again.

A second later the head of a merboy appears. He has shell-encrusted skin, weed tangled in his hair, and his chest and shoulders are covered in intricate tattoos. He looks at us, one at a time, his jet-black eyes lingering on me and Rose. The gills at the side of his neck open and close with a wet slurping sound. Then he says something that sounds a bit like, "Feesh meester splish?"

"Well, go on, Rose," says Win. "Ask him."

Rose looks at Win properly for the first time today. "Ask him what?"

"To pull the boat."

She gives an exasperated laugh. "How can I ask him that? I don't speak Mermish, or whatever weird language he was speaking in."

"Yes, you do!" says Win encouragingly. "You're fluent."

"No, *I'm not*." Then Rose presses her lips together as if she's scared a few words of Mermish might pop out.

"Fine. Keep rowing, then," says Win, and he lies back on the bench, kicks off his sneakers, and dangles his bare feet over the side of the boat.

"Just try, Rose," I say. "The minute I arrived in Roar loads of stuff came back to me. Maybe it's the same with you and . . . Mermish."

"Fine!" Rose scowls at me, then moves closer to the merboy and starts whispering to him using lots of ishy-wishy words. It sounds just like one of the pretend languages we used to make up when we were little, but it can't be nonsense because the merboy is nodding his head and whispering back to her.

Suddenly Rose turns to me. "Arthur, give me your socks."

"Why?"

"He wants your socks. I don't know why."

"But he's not got feet!"

"Look, do you want to go to the Tangled Forest or not?"

"Yeah, Arthur," pipes up Win. "What do you like more, your socks or your grandad?"

With a sigh I take off my socks and hold them over the edge of the boat. The merboy's fingers close around them and he disappears with them under the water.

"Great," I say. "He's gone, and now I've not got my watch or any—"

With a sudden lurch the boat shoots forward. I manage to grab on, but Win slams back into the jars between the seats. "MER-POWER!" he cries as the merboy swims ahead of us, a rope held tightly in his sock-encased fist.

The boat picks up speed, bumping over the waves and sending water spraying over us. Then I feel something bash against us. A moment later, a sleek silver tail flips out of the water and then a webbed hand grips the side of the boat, followed by another and another. I look around and realize that the water is packed full of mermaids and merboys all propelling us forward.

Win scrambles back onto the bench as we fly over the surface of the sea. "What did you say to him, Rose?" I shout.

She turns around and her hair whips across her face. "I said I was Rose Trout, Master of Roar, and that we'd come back to save Roar and needed his help."

"WAHOOOO!" screams Win. "HEAR HER ROAR!" He attempts to high-five her, but she just scowls and bats him away like he's an annoying fuzzy.

CHAPTER 26

We're pulled in Mitch's boat on a winding journey through the Archie Playgo and then out across the Bottomless Ocean. The sea isn't wild here like it is around the Crow's Nest, but it's still rough, and the three of us are forced to huddle together as waves hit us on all sides. The bumping and bouncing stops when we leave the Bottomless Ocean and sail up a wide river.

We see the Tangled Forest way before we reach it. It's a mighty wall of trees that rises up and dominates the skyline. The merfolk stay with us, pushing Mitch's boat closer and closer to the forest until the trees tower over us, their leaves blocking out the sunlight.

One by one the merfolk slip away, until just the first merboy is left pulling our boat. "I hope he knows what he's doing," I say, gripping the side of the boat as we race toward the wide trunks.

"Look!" Rose points to a dark gap between the trees almost hidden by trailing leaves. The river seems to disappear into it, and at the last possible moment the merboy lets go of the rope and shoves us toward the gap. Then, with a wave of his hand, and my watch and my socks, he gets ready to swim away.

"Wait!" I shout. If my fidget spinner let Win get into Home, then why not my socks or watch? What if everything

that comes from Home has this power? It's a risk I just can't take. The merboy stares at me with shining black eyes. "I'm sorry," I say, "but I really need my stuff back!"

Rose glares at me. "Let him keep it, Arthur. I made a deal with him!"

But I ignore her. "Please," I say to the merboy. "I have to have them back. It's important."

Seconds later my wet socks fly through the air followed by my watch. The merboy aims well: everything hits me hard in the face. I'm rubbing my stinging cheek when he raises his hand for a final wave before diving down into the water.

Rose sighs with irritation. "Arthur, what could be so important about a dirty pair of socks and a cheap watch?"

I'm about to explain, but then our boat slips between the towering trees of the Tangled Forest. The blue sky disappears and darkness wraps around us. Suddenly Home and Grandad's attic seem very far away.

"I'll tell you later," I whisper as we float into a strange and shadowy place. Creepers and vines twist between the trees like vast webs, and glowing buds blink in the darkness. Leaves seem to tremble for no reason and a curious oozing, dripping sound fills the air along with the clicks of hidden insects.

"This place is creepy," whispers Rose.

"I like it," I say.

I might hate heights, but the dark doesn't bother me at all. It's still in here and peaceful, a bit like a cathedral lit by flickering candles. Caught on some invisible current, Mitch's little boat carries us deeper and deeper into the forest.

Eventually the river disappears between the roots of an immense tree and we can't go any farther. "We have to walk now," says Win.

We climb out of the boat and scramble up the bank.

The height of the trees makes me dizzy, and when I look up I can only see the tiniest pinpricks of light breaking through the leaves. Down on the dark forest floor paths crisscross each other and the glowing buds stretch into the distance. Suddenly I realize how hard it's going to be to find the Lost Girls. I feel like we're moving away from Grandad and the Crow's Nest, not closer.

"This place is *massive*," I say. "How do we even know which path to take? We could be searching for the Lost Girls for days!"

Win strides toward a narrow track. "It's this way!"

"How do you know?" says Rose.

"Because I read the sign." He pushes back a vine and we see a wooden sign nailed to a tree. "THE LOST GIRLS" is painted on it in wobbling brushstrokes along with an arrow. "And look, there's another one!" He points to a tree farther along the path.

"Then I suppose we follow the signs," says Rose, and although this seems suspiciously easy to me we all head off along the path.

As we walk farther into the forest Win practices his stealth walk. This involves him trotting from tree to tree on tiptoe. Every now and then he says, "Can you see me?" and we look up to see him standing very still in front of a tree with his hands in front of his face.

"Yes," says Rose each time.

"Not really," I say to make him feel better.

Soon we're hot and sweaty and the Lost Girls' signs have become much harder to follow. Vines twist in ever thicker tangles between the trees and we're reduced to climbing over and under things to keep going. And the signs pop up in the strangest of places: at the top of a tree, in the middle of a hollow log. We even find one submerged in a murky pond.

As we wade through the water it's hard to shake the feeling that the Lost Girls are playing an elaborate trick on us.

Eventually we get to a sign that suggests we have to go through the middle of some brambles.

"No way," says Rose. "I'm not doing it."

Win examines the bush before dropping down on his stomach and wriggling underneath it. "Hurry up," he calls from the other side. "You've got to see this!"

I go next, and when I pull myself out Win is already halfway across a rope bridge that stretches across a ravine. The bridge is long, droops down in the middle, and is made up of battered planks of wood tied together with fraying rope.

Before I follow Win, I peer down into the ravine. Below I see the river with the rainbow shine that runs through Roar. Lime-green crystals cover the riverbed, making the water glow in the darkness of the forest. Chunks of crystal stick out like jagged teeth with water foaming and crashing around them. I pull out the map and see that the river cuts through the middle of the Tangled Forest and leads directly into the Bad Side.

"Come on, Arthur!" calls Win, deliberately wobbling the bridge. "This is fun!"

The moment my feet make contact with the planks the bridge starts to swing even more wildly from side to side. I hold on tight to the handrails. "This thing does not feel safe!"

"It's fine," says Win, and he jumps up and down to prove his point.

Just then Rose scrambles out from under the bush and joins us on the bridge. We start to walk along in a straggling line.

"One thing I don't get," I say, trying to ignore the alarming gaps between each plank, "is the signs. The Lost Girls are into hiding, right?"

"They're a guerrilla unit," says Rose. "They train in secret, then commit daring ambushes and raids." She *almost* sounds excited as she says this. Rose loved the Lost Girls and was always trying to persuade me to go looking for them.

"But that's what I mean: guerrilla units hide out and the Lost Girls have retreated deep into this forest, so I guess they don't want to be found."

"What's your point?" says Rose.

"My point *is*, why would they put up loads of signs telling us how to find them? Don't you think this could be a trap?"

Up ahead, Win stops walking. "*That* is a very good point, Arthur."

And at that moment a shrill giggle makes us turn around.

Standing at the start of the bridge is a little girl. She looks young, about six years old, and she has bare feet and is wearing a yellow T-shirt and shorts. She stands there staring at us and sucking at the end of her braid.

"Hello," says Rose, breaking the silence.

The girl smiles shyly.

"Is she a Lost Girl?" I ask Win.

He shrugs. "I don't know . . . she looks a bit clean."

"Maybe she's lost her way in the forest," says Rose, then she calls back to the girl, "Do you want to come with us? Do you want us to take you home?"

But the girl's not listening. She's taken something out of her pocket and is busy fiddling about with the ropes of the bridge.

"What's she doing?" asks Win.

I shade my eyes from the sun, but the girl is standing in the shadows of the trees and it's hard to see what she's up to.

"She's got something in her hand," says Rose. "I think it's a . . . *penknife!*"

That's when I see the blade glinting in the sun and realize Rose is right. The girl's got a knife and she's calmly using it to saw at the ropes of the bridge!

Suddenly one of the handrails droops. "Run!" cries Rose. "RUN!"

We turn and start running, heading for safety on the other side of the bridge. But the girl's knife must be sharp, and she must be stronger than she looks, because first one handrail goes slack, and then the other. They slip from my hands and I fall to my knees and grab hold of a plank. Below me water tumbles over the rocks. I can't crawl. I can't move at all. The bridge is wobbling too much.

"HOLD ON!" screams Rose, and that's when I feel the bridge collapse beneath me.

I wrap my arms even tighter around the plank as we hurtle toward the side of the ravine. I brace myself just in time, then we slam into rock and thick trailing plants. Twigs scratch my face and my knuckles are bashed, but somehow I cling on as the bridge bounces once, twice, then comes to a stop.

I'm frozen with shock, my whole body trembling, but I manage to get my feet up onto a plank. Up above, I see Win do the same, scrabbling to find a footing. The bridge is resting against the side of the ravine and has become a ladder—a dangly, unstable, terrifying ladder. Then I remember Rose.

I look down and see that she must have slipped when we hit the wall of the ravine. She's hanging off the very end of the bridge with one arm hooked around a plank and her legs swinging in thin air.

I open my mouth to speak, but no words come out.

Rose looks up at me with wide eyes.

"MASSIVE HEAD RUSH!" shouts Win, and his laughter echoes across the ravine.

Rose just hangs there, hugging her plank. "I think I'm going

to puke," she calls up to us, "or fall, but I don't know which I'm going to do first."

I swallow. "Just . . . hang on," I say. For someone who's afraid of heights, dangling over a ravine is about the worst thing that can happen. A cold lump of fear has formed inside me, and right now I can't think about helping Rose. The only thing I can do is concentrate on not freaking out. The bridge creaks, and dust and stones fall down on us.

Rose yelps and I shut my eyes and wait for the rocks to stop falling. When I open them again I look back across the ravine.

The sweet little girl who just tried to kill us gives me a wave, then vanishes into the forest.

CHAPTER 27

"Now don't panic . . . ," says Win, his voice echoing down to us, "but it looks like the ropes holding up the bridge might snap at any moment!"

I panic big-time. Waves of fear run through my body, from my scalp to my toes.

"I mean, I don't know for certain . . . ," he continues, "but they look a bit . . . breaky."

I force myself to breathe in slowly through my nose, then blow out through my mouth. Mum taught me to do this whenever I feel anxious, although I think she was imagining I'd use it in situations like losing my water bottle or forgetting my homework, rather than dangling over a ravine.

Amazingly Mum's breathing technique actually works, so I do it again and again until I'm able to look down at Rose and give her a reassuring smile.

I don't get one back.

"I've got an idea," Win shouts.

He sounds so confident that a glimmer of hope creeps into me. "What is it?"

"There's a chance I can use my magic to mend the bridge, but I'll need some extra energy to do it. I need you two to say: *We believe in Win-magic.*"

"Really?" I look up. "We just have to say those words?"

"Yep."

Quickly I call out, "We believe in Win-magic!"

"You too, Rose," says Win.

"We believe in Win-magic!" Her voice sounds faint.

Win pulls out his wand and I grip the ropes tighter, preparing for an explosion or a giant puff of smoke . . . but nothing happens. "Sorry," says Win. "I think the magic will only work if you say it together *with enthusiasm.*"

"WE BELIEVE IN WIN-MAGIC!" we both yell, making the bridge tremble and more dust fall on us.

When the dust settles and the bridge is still again I notice two things: we are still hanging over the ravine and Win is chuckling. "Gotcha!"

"What?" I shout. "*What?!*"

"It was a joke," he says, still laughing. "No way is my magic good enough to mend a bridge!"

"Right," I say, trying and failing to control my voice. "We've just wasted possibly the last minutes of our lives on Win's joke. Now what? How do we get off this bridge alive?"

"Arthur," Rose calls, "you're always making stuff up. You've got a telescope. You think of something!"

"Are you ever going to stop going on about the telescope?"

"Look, I'm not sure how much longer I can do this. I'm kind of counting on you, Arthur."

I hear the fear in her voice and I understand what she's saying. Win is incapable of taking anything seriously, and a bit incapable generally, and Rose is putting all her energy into holding on. This is *all* up to me. So I think. I think in a random way about weights and forces and pendulums, until I come up with something that's fractionally better than nothing.

"We need to climb up one at a time. If we go together, then the bridge will swing around and the ropes might snap. When Win gets to the top there will be less weight and he can hold the bridge steady while I climb. Then we both hold it still for you, Rose."

"Good plan," she says, and amazingly she isn't being sarcastic. "Go on, Win, but go *slowly*."

"I have been training for this for years," he says, and then he starts to climb the broken bridge, muttering, "*Creepy, creepy, slowly, slowly!*"

The bridge wobbles, and I hold my breath until Win shouts down, "I've done it. I'm off the bridge! But you need to hurry up, Arthur. The ropes do not look good!"

His words fill me with adrenaline and I'm suddenly so pumped I reckon I could get up and off this bridge in seconds. But then I remember Rose. When I look down I see that she has a look of grim determination on her face and she's trying to pull her feet up onto a plank . . . but she can't do it. The gaps between the planks are too big. She can't reach. Soon her arms are wobbling and her fingers are white from the pressure of holding on. How is she going to climb up the bridge if she can't pull herself up?

I start to climb—only instead of going up, I go down.

"Arthur, what are you doing?" yells Win.

I don't reply. I keep my eyes focused on Rose and try to turn the rapids below us into a blur.

Rose stares back up at me. "If you're trying to be some sort of hero, Arthur, don't bother, because you're literally the least heroic person I know. . . ."

But I know my sister. She hates admitting that she needs or wants my help, so I keep going until I'm close enough to reach out my hand. "Take it," I say.

After a moment's hesitation she reaches up and grabs hold of it. Keeping my free arm wrapped around a plank, I pull as hard as I can. I can't help thinking of all the times Rose has beaten me in arm wrestles. Maybe she's been training me up for this moment. Just when it feels like my arm might snap Rose lunges forward, gets her fingers around a higher plank, and swings her feet onto the bottom rung of the bridge.

For a moment the two of us cling to the bridge as it sways. My arm throbs and my chest heaves as I fight to get my breathing under control.

"HURRY UP!" yells Win, and then something red zooms past my head.

"Let's go," says Rose. "Together."

"What, like a twin thing?"

She shakes her head. "Nothing as dorky as that. Just a . . . brother and sister thing."

With Rose below me we start to climb, our hands and feet moving in time so that the bridge stays as still as possible. We don't talk, we just work together, and soon we're getting close to the top.

"Guys, the rope is like a string . . . no, a *thread!*" shouts Win. "HURRY UP!"

"Hold on to it!" I yell.

"I'm trying . . . I'm trying, but it's slipping through my fingers!" We feel the bridge drop slightly and some rocks tumble past us. Then Win starts crying out, "ROPE BURN . . . ROPE BURN!" and Rose and I climb as fast as we can, getting closer and closer to Win's pain-stricken face.

With a final burst of effort, I pull myself over the edge of the ravine, scramble next to Win, then reach down and grab Rose's arm. Win takes hold of her other arm and we start to heave. Before her feet are on solid land the ropes snap. We pull Rose up just as the bridge crashes down into the river. Then the three of us stand in a trembling line, legs shaking, hearts hammering, and watch as planks smash on the rocks and ropes are sucked under the foaming water.

Win throws his arms around our shoulders. "Did you see my magic? I magicked you up an inner tube in case you didn't make it!"

"You mean that red thing that flew past us?" Rose shakes her head. "It could have killed us, Win."

"But still"—Win's eyes go wide—"*an inner tube.*"

"Pretty amazing," I say.

He sighs. "It was better than amazing, Arthur; it was *imaginary!*"

Rose catches my eye and grins. She must be in shock because that is the first joke we've shared in months. And then she does another first. She turns and looks at Win, and I mean properly looks at him, and says, "Thank you for trying to hold on to the bridge, Win."

"Anything for the Masters of Roar," he says, squeezing us close.

When he lets us go we stare across the deep ravine.

"That girl . . ." Rose shakes her head. "I thought she was cute. I wanted to help her!"

"That's the Lost Girls for you," says Win. "And now I guess we're going to have to keep following their deadly signs."

"But they led us to the bridge," I say.

Rose shrugs. "What choice do we have? We can't go back the way we came."

She's right. There's no bridge now. We're trapped in this half of the Tangled Forest.

"I wonder what the Lost Girls have got planned for us next?" I say.

"Something painful," says Win, "and very surprising."

And that's when a twig snaps behind us, my arms are yanked behind my back, and something rough is thrown over my head. Next my hands are bound so tightly I cry out. The screams and shouts coming from each side tell me that Win and Rose are being tied up too.

Everything goes quiet, then Win says, "I, for one, found that very surprising."

"Quiet," snaps a small, hard voice. "Stella wants a word with you, and if she doesn't like what you've got to say, you'll get smashed up, just like that bridge at the bottom of the ravine!" She ends her speech by doing a mad, gurgling laugh, and the rest of our captors join in too.

This demonic giggling, combined with the fact that it's coming from somewhere below my shoulders, tells me that we've finally found the Lost Girls.

"Well," says Rose as small fingers prod my back, forcing me to start walking, "this is what we wanted to happen."

"I guess," I say, and then a foot kicks the backs of my knees, sending me tumbling to the ground.

"Nice one, Audrey!" squeals a voice. "He fell in bird poo. LOADS OF IT!" and then they start laughing all over again.

CHAPTER 28

After a long, hot walk through the forest, my arms are untied and the hood is yanked off my head.

I find myself staring at a red-haired girl who has a mean expression. An elaborate collection of loom-band bracelets are arranged up both of her wrists and she's chewing on a twig . . . no, a bone.

She takes out the bone, reaches up, and prods me with it in the middle of my forehead. "State your business, *boy!*" She looks eight, nine at the most, but her steely eyes belong to someone much older.

"Yes . . . ," I say, blinking into the sunshine, "our business . . ."

She's flanked by a pack of girls who look similarly grubby and tough. Each of them has bracelets on their wrists, but none has anywhere near as many as their leader.

"Hey, *boy!*" Another girl steps forward and shoves me in the chest. She has to shove me in the chest; she can't reach any higher. "When Stella speaks, you reply!"

A quick glance at Rose tells me that that she's decided to leave all the talking to me, so I blurt out, "Crowky's taken our grandad and we need you to help us rescue him!"

"Oh, do you?" Stella says, eyebrows raised, and the other Lost Girls collapse in giggles.

"Yes we do," I say, then I stand a little taller. "Do you know who we are?"

"I know who you are all right. You're Arthur and Rose Trout, *Masters of Roar*." She says these last words with a sarcastic curl of her lip.

"Don't speak to them like that," protests Win. "They're here to help us!"

Stella glares at him. "Crowky has been terrorizing us for ages and they just left him to it. We haven't seen them for over two years!"

"It's actually been three years, three months, and twenty-one days," says Win, helpfully.

Stella's eyes narrow and she turns back to me. "And you think you can come back here and demand our help? I'll admit that Crowky is a total pain in the bum"—there are murmurs of agreement from the other girls—"but we're not scared of him and he doesn't bother us anymore." She throws her arms out wide. "Not now that we've got our awesome camp. We're safe here. We've got our hammocks and our fire. Why should we risk all this for your grandad?"

"Yeah!" snarl the other girls.

A girl with braids and a bow slung over her shoulder shouts out, "Where were the Masters of Roar when Crowky stuffed Stella and trashed Treetops? It took Stella weeks to recover and we loved that camp!"

Now all the girls are jeering at us, and calling us names like *dum-dum heads* and *pea-brains* and stepping closer and closer. A collection of motley weapons appears in their hands—sticks and homemade bows and arrows.

"If Crowky doesn't bother you," I say quickly, "then how come you're hiding out in this forest and trying to chuck people down ravines? It looks to me like he's bothering you *a lot.* It looks to me like you're scared of him!"

Stella goes white and then red, then she grabs hold of my T-shirt and pulls me down toward her face. "Say that again, *poo head!*"

"Ha! *Poo head!*" cries Win, forgetting for a moment whose side he's on.

Over Stella's shoulder I catch a glimpse of the Lost Girls' "awesome camp." It's nothing more than some ratty hammocks stretched between trees, a smoldering fire, and a lot of puddles. Then I have a moment of inspiration. "Help us get rid of Crowky, and the Crow's Nest is yours!"

"Interesting . . ." Stella shoves me back into the mud and beckons the other girls over. They gather in a huddle, arms thrown around each other's shoulders. After a few minutes of intense whispering, Stella turns to face me. "We accept, Arthur Trout, but on one condition."

"What's that?"

"*I'm* in charge." She jabs a thumb at her chest. "The Lost Girls take orders from me, and only me."

"Fine, you can be our leader—"

"Chief."

I nod. "OK, chief."

Stella grins. "Actually there is one other condition."

"What is it?" I ask.

"We want you to roll around on the ground and pretend to be a baby."

All the Lost Girls start laughing.

"What?!"

"You heard me," says Stella. "Roll around on the ground and pretend to be a baby!"

"Just do it, Arthur," says Rose.

"*You* just do it!"

"No," says Stella. "No girls. We only want the boys to do it."

"Cool!" says Win, then he drops down to the ground and starts to scream and wave his arms and legs around.

The Lost Girls clap with delight, then look at me and start chanting, "Do it! Do it!" until I get down next to Win and join in. When they're all whooping and cheering and their weapons are being put away Rose pulls us to our feet, not even bothering to hide the smile on her face.

"Now you've got to hear Rose's plan," I say. "I promise you, it's good."

Stella rolls her eyes. "Fine. Tell us your stupid plan."

After Rose has spoken, Stella has to admit that it's not "totally dumb." "We'll attack the Crow's Nest the day after tomorrow," she says.

I shake my head. "No. That's too late. Grandad's stuffed and unless we can get there quickly he could stay stuffed!"

Stella just shrugs. "I don't care. I want my girls to get there alive. This Magic Road sounds treacherous, and if we're going to stay hidden from Crowky until the last moment, we're going to have to approach the castle in the dark, so we'll need to train. We'll use your map to re-create the Magic

Road right here in the Tangled Forest. And there's another thing."

"What?" I say.

"You lot are coming along that Magic Road with us. You've done it before and you can help. Plus, why should we risk our lives getting to the Crow's Nest and fighting the scarecrows while you three sneak in the back door on dragons?"

Rose, Win, and I gather together. "She's got a point," says Rose.

I nod. "And we should just have time. Crowky said that he stuffed Grandad yesterday, which means we've still got two days to get to him."

"It feels risky," says Rose, "but what choice do we have? We need them to help us."

I pull out the map. "There's this rock, here"—I point at a large rock Win drew—"it looks big and it's close to the castle. If we arrive there at dawn, Rose can whistle for the dragons and they can pick us up and take us to the sea cave from there."

"That should work," says Win.

Rose looks at Stella. "We'll do it. Today Arthur and Win can learn to ride a dragon and tomorrow we'll train. Then we'll cross the Magic Road together."

Stella studies us for a moment, then nods and turns to her girls. "Flora, Hannah"—two girls step forward and puff out their chests—"you're in charge of weapon-sharpening.

Shania and Hansini—you lead the other girls on a five-mile jog." Groans break out among the girls, but Stella silences them with a look. "And later this afternoon I want to see you all doing hand-to-hand combat, and I'm not talking slaps. Those scarecrows are nasty and fast and there are loads of them, so we're going to have to do actual punching and karate chops."

"Oh . . . oh!" Win practically jumps up and down. "I can help with that."

Stella narrows her eyes. "No. You can't." She turns back to her girls. "Then we'll build our very own Magic Road ready for training in the morning. Clear?"

"Yes, chief!" The girls salute, then spread out across the camp.

Stella leads us back into the forest. She explains that they have a dojo, a place where they practice wrestling, which she thinks will be perfect to land a dragon. "This is where we'll build the Magic Road," she says as we come out on a round, flat clearing.

We blink into the sunshine. The dojo is high above Roar, and over the miles and miles of trees, I can just see the glimmer of the Bottomless Ocean and beyond that, the snowy mountains of the End. I turn in a circle and realize that we're probably at the very heart of the Tangled Forest.

The crack that appeared on our birthday is here too, cutting across the dojo. It's not quite big enough to fall down, but stepping over it is still unnerving.

"Hey, Stella," says Rose. "Can I ask you something?"

"*Chief* Stella."

"Right, Chief Stella. Have you seen Mitch around? She's a mermaid-witch, about my height, blue hair . . . magical tail."

"And a bad temper?" says Stella.

"That's her!"

Stella shakes her head. "I bumped into her down at the Archie Playgo about a year ago. We had a fight over some mushrooms." Her scowl suggests Mitch might have won.

Rose nods and scuffs her foot into the dusty dojo. "And you've not seen her since?"

"No, but a lot of things have gone missing since you stopped visiting. Maybe she disappeared down the crack." To emphasize her point, Stella takes a rock and chucks it into the split in the ground.

"Or Mitch could be out in the Archie Playgo," I say quickly. "Or maybe she went to the End."

Rose doesn't say anything; she turns on her heel and walks to the far side of the dojo. Then she puts her fingers to her lips and does a quick whistle, just like you'd use to call a dog. This is how Rose always used to summon the dragons, and as long as she was standing outside it seemed to work every time.

The four of us gaze at the empty sky and my stomach squirms as I think about my journey dangling from Pickle's claws. I'm wondering if Rose's whistle has worked when I see two specks on the horizon. The dragons shoot through the air, covering miles in seconds, beating a path straight toward us. Sweat prickles my skin and I take a couple of deep breaths. I nudge Win. "You reckon we can do this? You and me? Learn how to fly a dragon?"

Ahead of us, Pickle snaps at his brother and Vlad retaliates with a nip at Pickle's tail. Suddenly they're tumbling through the sky and the air is torn apart by their screeches; Pickle clamps down on a wing tip and a jet of fire shoots from Vlad's jaws.

"Should be pretty easy," says Win, stepping back from the flames. "Like riding a horse, I reckon. Or a unicorn."

"Have you ever ridden a horse or a unicorn?"

"No, have you?" he asks. I shake my head. "Oh well, riding a dragon's probably more like riding a bike, and we've done that loads of times. Our dragon-riding skills are going to be imaginary, Arthur!"

Next to me, Rose snorts.

CHAPTER 29

The dragons land in a tangle of wings and fire and rage, but Rose doesn't hesitate. She strides over, dodges around their lashing tails, and forces them apart by slapping at their snouts. "Bobad boboys, bobad boboys!" she shouts, then when they're cowering by her feet, she beckons us over.

"Here goes," says Win, thumping me on the arm. "Let's take these dragons to school!" Then he frowns. "What even *is* school?"

"I'll tell you some other time."

Rose passes me a handful of broken cookies. "Give these to Vlad. You need to gain his trust by feeding him."

"Vlad? Why can't we fly Pickle?"

"Arthur, just because Vlad has got a scary name, doesn't mean he's the scariest dragon."

"Yeah, but he is, isn't he?" I eye Vlad's wide blue bulk. He seems much more sinister than rosy-red Pickle.

"Vlad's big-boned, that's all," she says. "Now get over there while he's still worn out from his fight."

I take a deep breath, blow out nice and slow, then walk toward Vlad. He's hunkered down, licking a drop of black blood from a tear in his wing. His tongue is thick and gray and has fiery cracks running through it like molten magma. When he sees me stepping closer his head rises, his lips pull back, and his yellow eyes narrow to slits. "Here, Vlad," I say, my voice wobbling, "come and get a cookie." I reach out my hand and his mouth opens to reveal a set of large needle-sharp teeth. Smoke begins to seep from his nostrils.

"Careful, Arthur," says Rose as I hold out the cookies. "You've got to put them right in his mouth. If you chuck them in, he'll know you're scared. Dragons don't respect you if they think you're scared of them."

I put my hand up to protect my face from the heat that's

radiating from Vlad and inch closer. He's getting impatient now, snapping hungrily around my hand, so I reach forward as far as I dare and drop in the cookies. They fall down his fiery gullet and he tosses his head back, gnashing his teeth enthusiastically.

"Now's your chance!" says Rose. "Get on his back. You too, Win!"

"How?" I circle Vlad's bulging body.

"Climb him. Imagine he's one of those models at the Dinotastic Play Park."

Amazingly Rose's shoddy advice works, and I'm able to scramble up Vlad's side by pretending he's made of fiberglass. I pull myself into a sitting position by grabbing hold of one of the spikes that line his back. Immediately I shift from side to side. Vlad's scales are roasting; this is like sitting on the embers of a bonfire! I feel bones and muscles moving beneath Vlad's scaly skin and he turns his head and glowers at me.

I sit as still as possible, until he looks away.

Win pulls himself up behind me and settles down. "Right," he says, rubbing his hands with enthusiasm, or possibly because he just burned them, "how do we fly this thing?"

And that's when I realize we should have found this out *before* we climbed onto Vlad's back. "Rose!" I shout. "Tell us what to do!"

She cups her hands around her mouth and calls, "It's

easy! Squeeze with your left knee to go left and your right knee to go right. Oh, and say 'robise' to make him go up!"

"Rub eyes?" says Win.

"No, *robise!*"

"*Robise?!*" Win bellows, and instantly Vlad's crusty ears prick up and his immense wings expand. Before Win and I can even think of escaping, Vlad has heaved his body to standing and begun a lolloping jog across the dojo.

The ground shakes and Win and I hold tight to the spikes. I bounce up and down, my bum slamming repeatedly into his rough, hot scales. "How do we get him to land?" I shout to Rose.

She says something that might be "dobdob" or "hobnob," but I can't hear over Vlad's thudding wings.

"Rose! What did you say?"

But it's too late. Vlad has reached the edge of the dojo and is taking a clumsy leap. Just when I think we're going to crash into the trees, his wings thrust down and we rise up in the air. I slip to one side as I look over my shoulder. "Rose!" I yell. "We don't know what we're doing!"

But she's not even looking in my direction. Instead she's settled herself on the dojo, resting against Pickle . . . I think she might be sunbathing!

Win leans forward. "Arthur, we're flying a dragon!" I swallow and nod, and squeeze my legs around Vlad's fat body as we soar higher and higher and farther away from Rose. Win laughs in delight. "Doesn't it feel dangerous?"

CHAPTER 30

"Make him go upside down, Arthur!"

"*No.*" I'm sitting with a straight back, my hands wrapped around the spike and my eyes fixed on the horizon. Wind whistles past my face as we rise up and down with each thrust of Vlad's wings. If I don't look down, I can almost pretend this is a computer game and nothing bad can possibly happen to me.

Win slaps his hands on my shoulders. "Make him fly into a volcano. That would be incredible!"

As we fly over Roar, Win keeps making reckless suggestions and I keep ignoring them, sticking to going left and right. We glide over a lake, then I squeeze my left knee and we swing over a forest. I press my right knee and we're back over the lake. A red bird flies alongside us for a while until Vlad growls at it, smothering it in smoke.

"That's it," I say, patting Vlad's craggy scales. "Ignore the bird and keep going. Good boy."

"Mate, you've got left and right nailed," says Win. "Try

something else. The day after tomorrow we've got to fly into a narrow tunnel, but right now all we can do is go in circles."

"I'm going straight now. Look." We've reached the Bottomless Ocean and are soaring across it, heading toward the horizon. "Anyway, Rose's lesson was useless."

Win leans forward and stares down at the sea. "I guess she wasn't expecting Vlad to take off like that."

I'm not in the mood to hear Win defend Rose. "Win, by the time we left the ground she was sunbathing. I can't believe she didn't come after us on Pickle. A few hours ago we saved her life, but now she sends us up into the sky on a . . . dangerous beast without thinking about our safety. Rose doesn't care about anyone except herself."

Win shakes his head. "That's not true. Rose has *always* been there when we've needed her. Remember what happened at the Crow's Nest?!"

"You've not seen her at home, Win. Trust me. She's changed."

We fly on in silence for a few minutes, then Win says, "I don't know about what Rose is like in Home, but she's always looked out for you here. She must know you can handle this, otherwise she would have come after us."

Win's words make me think and sit up a little taller. Could he be right? Could Rose not being by my side be a good thing, not a bad thing?

"Look, Arthur." Win points down to where a massive lump of rock rises out of the sea. Waves have hollowed out its middle, forming a narrow archway. "*That* would be perfect tunnel-flying practice."

"Don't you think it's a bit small?"

"No . . . well, *yes*, but Mitch always went on about how small and narrow the sea cave was so we should give it a go."

Win's right. For the mission, for saving Grandad, we *should* give it a go. Only I'm frightened of doing anything that could make us fall off Vlad's back. No, not frightened, petrified. The idea of tumbling through the sky makes me feel helpless and sick, like I'm already falling.

We're closer to the rock now and I can see waves being sucked into the archway. If Vlad is going to fit through there, we'll have to go fast and at an angle. All we've got to hold on to are spikes, and right now my spike is slippery with sweat. I shake my head. "Sorry, Win. It's too dangerous."

He gives a cry of exasperation. "Mate, you're Arthur Trout, *Master of Roar*! How can you fight Crowky if you're scared of flying through a hole?"

Win's words burn into me. They make me stare straight ahead, heart thumping, cheeks flushed. Not because I'm angry, but because I know he's right. If I'm ever going to see Grandad again, I need to stop thinking about all the ways I could slip, fall, or tumble, and start to believe I can do this . . . on my own.

I came to Roar, didn't I? I climbed down that bridge to get to Rose, and right now I'm sitting on a dragon! I don't take my eyes off the rocky archway as Vlad's heat rises up through me. What was Rose shouting when we took off? It sounded like gobbledygook . . .

No, not gobbledygook: Obby Dobby.

Obby Dobby was a made-up language that Grandad taught me and Rose. Only I never got it as well as them, and they used to drive me mad chatting away in it. Rose told us to say "robise" to make Vlad take off, which is the word *rise* with *ob* stuck in the middle of it. Could Obby Dobby be Rose's mysterious dragon language?

There's one way to find out.

I lean close to Vlad's ear, and yell, "*Dobown!*"

Instantly Vlad's head drops and he dives toward the sea. My stomach drops too as cold air races past us and we're flung back.

"YES!" screams Win.

I keep my eyes open, forcing myself to watch, and just before Vlad's snout touches a wave, I shout, "Globide!" He rears up and next thing I know, we're coasting smoothly over the Bottomless Ocean. I'm half blinded by sea spray and smoke, but I can just see the archway rising up out of the sea. I glance at Vlad's outspread wings. Can they possibly fit through the gap? I nudge him to the left, and then a little bit farther until he's flying at an angle. Win and I lean as far forward as we can, our knees pressed into Vlad's scaly sides.

"Do you reckon we're going to make it?" Win's voice sounds strangely . . . *scared.*

"Definitely," I say, then I fix my eyes on the gap as Vlad speeds up. We shoot into the archway and I'm blinded by smoke. Win screams, the dragon growls, then I see blue sky and realize I'm breathing fresh air . . . I did it. I flew Vlad through the archway and we survived!

"HEAR ME ROAR!" I cry, punching my fist in the air. Vlad breathes out a triumphant blaze of fire and his wings pound down, lifting us back up. While Win laughs hysterically, I wipe the sea spray from my face and stare at the Bottomless Ocean.

"Boback tobo Rose!" I command, and Vlad bellows his approval as he turns and heads for land.

It's a beautiful journey across Roar. The sun is setting, creating a glittering path on the sea for Vlad to follow. I can see the Archie Playgo and the Tangled Forest in front of us, a vast expanse of shifting, swaying trees.

Just when I'm thinking how wonderful it is to be here, flying over Roar and not feeling scared, I spot something ahead.

It looks like a swirling black cloud, which is strange, because we're in the Good Side, and there isn't another cloud in sight.

"What's that?" I point it out to Win.

"I dunno. It looks like . . . *birds*."

He's right. As Vlad flies closer I see that it isn't one thing—a cloud—but actually lots of birds—crows—huddled together and flying as one. They swoop up in the sky, turn, then pour down in our direction.

"Fobastober!" I shout. "FOBASTOBER!"

Vlad dives down, but so do the birds until they're surrounding us—a mass of black squawking feathers and pecking beaks—driving the dragon wild. I cover my face with one arm and lash out with the other. The birds are small, but there are so many of them I can't stop their claws and beaks from scratching and pecking at my skin.

Soon Vlad's had enough. He whips his head around, breathes out a jet of fire, and sends the birds fluttering in all directions, smoke drifting from their singed wings.

"What was that all about?" I say, brushing away feathers, and licking the blood from a deep scratch on my hand.

Win sweeps a pile of feathers off Vlad's back. "Spies of Crowky's, I reckon. I've seen them around before, swooping over the forest and following me on my bike."

Then I notice something on my lap. At first I haven't got a clue what it is, until I pick it up. It's a plastic carrot with a smiley face. Dangling from the carrot are two keys. I curl my fist around Grandad's community garden key ring.

"Those crows weren't spies," I say. "They were messengers."

CHAPTER 31

Vlad circles over the dojo.

"What are they doing?" says Win, peering down.

The Lost Girls have been busy since we left. They're scurrying about all over the dojo, rolling stones into place and digging up great mounds of earth. Their previously smooth training area now looks like a building site.

"Making the Magic Road. Look, there's the tunnel"—I point at a place near the trees where a girl's head is poking out from a tarpaulin—"and over there, where they're piling up earth, that's the big rock where the dragons are going to pick us up."

"Those girls might be small," says Win, "but they're strong . . . and fast."

He's right. We've only been gone a few hours, but already the Lost Girls have transformed the dojo, re-creating a rough outline of the Magic Road, making it spiral in on itself so they can fit it all in. And that's after going on a five-mile jog.

"There's just one problem," I say. "Where can we land Vlad?"

As Vlad glides down, getting closer and closer to the dojo, I try to direct him toward the place with the fewest girls in it. "Dobown," I urge, nudging him to the right, then right a bit more. "Dobown . . ."

It's all going smoothly. Vlad is preparing to land, talons outstretched, not too fast and not too slow, but then he sees Rose standing with Stella at the start of the Magic Road. He roars with delight, swings left, and plunges toward her. Win and I scream. Rose and Stella scream, then they throw themselves into a muddy ditch as Vlad crashes to earth.

Win and I shoot over Vlad's head, land with a thud, then slide into Rose and Stella's ditch.

"Arthur!" yells Rose, wiping muddy water from her face.

"Sorry, but *someone* forgot to tell me how to land!"

The Lost Girls creep forward, fascinated by the dragon and the sight of Chief Stella covered in mud.

"If any of you laugh," she says, squeezing muddy water from her vest, "I'll take away five of your bracelets and put you on toilet-pit cleaning duty for a week."

No one laughs. Except Win, and he doesn't stop until Stella gives him an arm burn.

Our crash landing does have one unexpected benefit. The ditch was being dug out to provide a realistic wateriness to the Magic Road, with the camp's water supply diverted to fill it. When Vlad heaves himself up and flies off to find Pickle, he leaves behind a vast crater that immediately starts to fill with water.

After consulting the map, Stella decides that the crater will become Big Leap, the point on the Magic Road where there's a huge gap between two rocks. Now we can all practice doing the jump, with a pool of water beneath us, just in case we don't make it.

By now it's almost dark, so Stella issues dinner and tidying-up instructions. "But not you three," she says, nodding at me, Win, and Rose. "You can stay up here and finish the rocks around Big Leap."

I'm exhausted and battered, but one look at Stella's determined face tells me there's no point arguing. If Rose is bothered about being stuck with me and Win, she doesn't complain. We watch the Lost Girls trudge into the Tangled Forest, then start adding rocks to the pile the girls have already made. Rose looks from me to Win. She takes in our burnt hair, our smoke-covered faces, and our bruises and cuts. "So what exactly happened to you two?"

I touch a particularly painful graze on my cheek. "We nearly died because someone told us to get on a dragon, but didn't tell us how to fly it."

Rose laughs. "Yeah, but you didn't die, did you?"

"We came close," I mutter, but then I can't help smiling. "We flew through this archway in a rock, Rose. . . . It was small, and we had to fly Vlad on his side. But we did it and it was incredible!"

She heaves a spade full of muddy soil over her shoulder and slaps it down. "I knew you could do it," she says.

I slip my fingers into my pocket and wrap them around the carrot key ring. I decide not to mention it to Rose. She just did a kind thing for me, so I can do a kind thing for her.

When it's totally dark we abandon our digging and go down to the camp. We all agree that we're starving and can't wait to eat. Rose is pretty certain Stella mentioned something about beans on toast, and suddenly there is nothing I want more than a sloppy pile of baked beans on buttery toast.

It turns out Stella actually said *bees on toast*, which is disappointing and very alarming until we're handed slabs of toast dripping with honey.

As we sit around the campfire, licking honey off our fingers, Stella talks about Crowky.

"At first he stole things—our food, our weapons—then he came with the scarecrow army and set fire to Treetops.

Luckily the girls were out hunting, but he caught me in my tree house and stuffed me, then left me for the girls to find." She shudders at the memory and digs a stick into the embers of the fire. "If he finds us here, I don't know what we'll do. I think he got really angry when he stopped flying."

I look up with surprise. "But he flew yesterday. He lifted me in the air."

"Well, I haven't seen him flying in ages," says Stella.

"Now I think about it, neither have I," says Win.

Stella shakes her head. "That's not good. If he's flying again, he could be anywhere."

Automatically everyone's eyes shift from the fire to the canopy of leaves above us. Then Stella breaks the silence. "Has he been to your cave, Win?"

"Nope, he can't find it because I use camouflage . . . and *magic*." Then he pulls out his wand and says, "Whistle fur!" A single white marshmallow bursts out of the end of his wand. I'm not sure who's more surprised—us or Win. He proceeds to toast the marshmallow in the flames of the fire, then eat it slowly, pulling strands of goo off with his fingers, ignoring the big hungry eyes of the Lost Girls.

"Do it again," says one of the smallest ones, Clara, tugging his sleeve. "That was awesome."

"Really?" Win is so surprised to have genuinely impressed someone with his magic that he fluffs his next spell and produces first a cherry tomato and then what looks like a bit of cheese. But after that he starts magicking up marshmallow after marshmallow, and the Lost Girls creep closer and closer to him, hands outstretched.

When Clara is eating her marshmallow she suddenly says, "Arthur, why are we saving this man?"

The question takes me by surprise. "Oh," I say, "because he's our grandad."

She scowls. "I know *that*, but why's he so important?"

I guess the word *Grandad* doesn't mean much to Clara or the other Lost Girls; the only family they have are each other. I wonder how I can possibly explain that without Grandad and his fun, and the endless games he let us play in the attic, there might never have been a Roar. I look at Rose for help, but she's staring intently into the fire.

Now all the Lost Girls are watching me, waiting for my answer. "Our grandad is important because he believes in magic," I say, then I stop talking. I have to. I have a lump in my throat and my eyes are watering. I could pretend it's because of the smoke from the fire, but I'd be lying.

"OK," says Clara, then she turns back to Win and holds out her hand for another marshmallow. Like Rose, I fall quiet, gazing at the flames until Stella announces that it's time for a wrestling bout.

Apparently this is something the Lost Girls do every night before they go to bed, and soon logs are pushed out of the way and two girls are selected and take up their positions.

I quickly discover that the Lost Girls take wrestling seriously and it's a good distraction from my thoughts of Grandad. As they hurl each other to the ground Stella circles them, offering tactical advice, like "Poke her in the eye, Nell!" and "Bite her, Flora, BITE HER!"

I notice Flora yells, "Hear me roar!" as she slams into Nell.

"See," I say, nudging Rose. "She doesn't think it's a lame thing to say."

Rose rolls her eyes. "Well, it is."

After the wrestling, there's a short ceremony in which a Lost Girl is given one of Stella's loom-band bracelets. The girl is small and has a long braid and is wearing a yellow T-shirt. I realize she's the girl who cut the ropes on the bridge. Presumably she's found her way back to camp and is now being rewarded for trying to kill us, but I still find myself joining in with the applause because she looks so proud when Stella slips the bracelet around her wrist.

Next it's cookies and tea, and then bed.

"Magic Road training tomorrow," says Stella, crunching thoughtfully on a cookie. "Then we'll travel to the start of the Magic Road during the night." She looks at Win. "You're sure about when it appears?"

He nods. "Twice a day: an hour before dawn, and again twelve hours later."

"So tomorrow we train, rest in the afternoon, then set off for the Bad Side." She looks around the fire, until her eyes settle on me and Rose. "Then we go to the Crow's Nest, fight Crowky, and get your grandad back."

She jumps to her feet, grabs Win's very last marshmallow, and announces: "Bedtime!"

CHAPTER 32

While the Lost Girls settle down in their camp, Win, Rose, and I go back to the dojo, where we've tied hammocks between the trees. The dragons have decided to sleep up there too and are curled together between the muddy rocks of the pretend Magic Road.

As more and more stars come out Win chatters on about how heroic we were riding Vlad, ignoring Rose's frequent requests to "Please, shut up!" Eventually he drops off and soon his snores are competing with the low rumbling coming from the dragons.

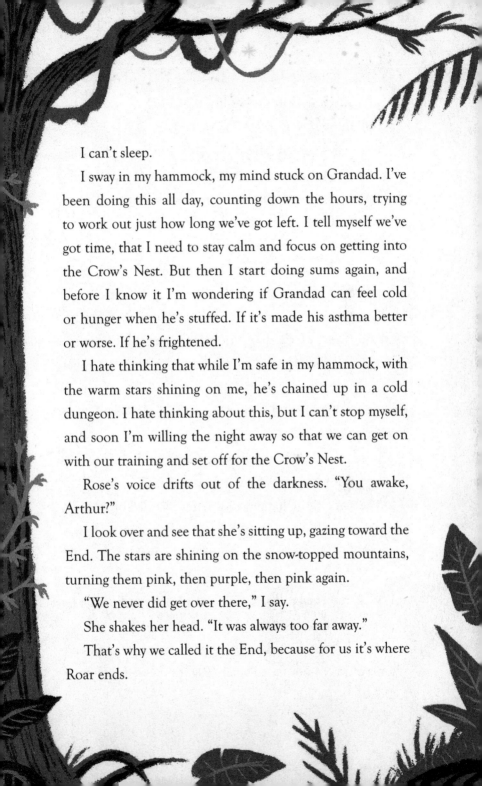

I can't sleep.

I sway in my hammock, my mind stuck on Grandad. I've been doing this all day, counting down the hours, trying to work out just how long we've got left. I tell myself we've got time, that I need to stay calm and focus on getting into the Crow's Nest. But then I start doing sums again, and before I know it I'm wondering if Grandad can feel cold or hunger when he's stuffed. If it's made his asthma better or worse. If he's frightened.

I hate thinking that while I'm safe in my hammock, with the warm stars shining on me, he's chained up in a cold dungeon. I hate thinking about this, but I can't stop myself, and soon I'm willing the night away so that we can get on with our training and set off for the Crow's Nest.

Rose's voice drifts out of the darkness. "You awake, Arthur?"

I look over and see that she's sitting up, gazing toward the End. The stars are shining on the snow-topped mountains, turning them pink, then purple, then pink again.

"We never did get over there," I say.

She shakes her head. "It was always too far away."

That's why we called it the End, because for us it's where Roar ends.

In the middle of the dojo a dragon growls and flames roll toward us. Sparks drift past us like fireflies.

"Still think this isn't real?" I say.

Rose stares straight ahead. "I can't. It's too frightening. People disappearing, the ground opening up, Crowky making an army and burning things down. We used to be in control of this place, but I don't know who's in control now." In the darkness I see her hug her knees. "I can't wait until we go home and can go back to forgetting this place ever existed."

The ground starts to shake, slowly at first, then harder, as if the roots of all the trees in the Tangled Forest are twisting and turning. My hands tighten around the ropes of the hammock as leaves fall on us and the dragons stir in their sleep. Suddenly I realize that exactly the same thing happened yesterday.

"Rose . . . I think you just made that happen."

She turns to face me. "What do you mean?"

"The same thing happened when we landed on Mitch's island: you said Roar wasn't real and straightaway there was an earth wobble, or whatever it was Win called it."

"So?"

"Well, just then you said you didn't believe in Roar and— boom—an earthquake hits."

"But . . . Roar isn't real, is it? Not like home. There aren't photos of it. It's not on any map. Right now we haven't got a clue where we are!"

There's a grumble of thunder, then a flash of lightning bursts from the sky and lands meters away from us. The dragons' eyes slide open and the hairs on my arms stand on end.

Rose lets out a long deep breath. "OK . . . that was strange. Shall I say something to test it out?"

"No! Don't even think it. If Roar comes from our imaginations, then maybe when we stop believing in it, it starts to fall apart and sinkholes open up and people . . . disappear."

Rose stares at me. "Are you saying that the things that have gone—Mitch, the mermaids, the unicorns—they went because I stopped believing in them?"

"I stopped believing in them too. Until I saw Win in the attic and found the map, I'd almost forgotten about Roar."

"But not totally?"

"No," I admit. "There's something else. Win said that big crack appeared on our birthday, at dusk, and we both know what happened then."

"The dragon fight . . . ," says Rose, and I nod.

I'd been out watching the new Star Wars film, and when I got back Rose announced that she'd had a clear-out and given Dad some toys to take to the charity shop. But they weren't any old toys. They were the models of dragons that we'd both been collecting for years.

"I flipped out," I say, remembering how I'd screamed in Rose's face, then charged into her room looking for things of hers that I could give away.

"Me too." Rose had run after me, thrown me to the ground, and sat on me.

"You said that you were never going to play with me again," I say.

"You said you hated me."

"And Roar nearly split in two."

For a moment we stare across Roar. One of the dragons rolls over. The dojo trembles.

"But it didn't," I say, "and we're here right now. . . . Doesn't that make you believe in Roar?"

"I can't. I want to go home!" She almost shouts the words. "I've changed. I'm not like you anymore, Arthur. I can't believe in any of this made-up stuff."

This time the ground shakes so hard that rocks crash down into the forest and birds rise up from the trees. The dragons wake up too. They huff and puff and send flames up into the sky to join the flashes of lightning that are exploding across Roar. Rose isn't saying she doesn't believe in Roar to be mean. She's just telling the truth. Rose does everything she can to fit in. Being able to crawl through a cot into a magical world isn't fitting in; it's the weirdest thing you could possibly do.

"I'm sorry, Arthur." I'm not sure if she's saying sorry for giving away the dragons, or for pulling apart our incredible world.

"It's OK." I curl up in my hammock. "We'll be home

soon. I promise." Then I pull the blanket over my shoulders.

Rose doesn't lie down. She stays where she is, staring across Roar to the End, the light from the stars shining on her face.

CHAPTER 33

"Right," says Stella, hands on hips. "Show us how it's done."

We're all gathered on the dojo, minus the dragons, who Rose has packed off for a fly over Roar to give us more room. For the past couple of hours we've been trying to get the fake Magic Road to resemble the real thing. This is tricky. Beyond the obvious problem of no sea, we only have what's in the Tangled Forest to help us, plus the map Win and I made, and our memories.

But as I study the bizarre obstacle course in front of me, I realize we haven't done a bad job. The most challenging parts of the road are all represented: the giant gaps between rocks, the tunnel, the narrow tightrope rock. We've even covered everything in soggy ferns to re-create the seaweed. We haven't made the last bit of the road, which no one has been along, and we're just hoping the Lost Girls don't get any nasty surprises when they reach it tomorrow.

"Ready?" I ask Win.

"Ready!" he cries, then he goes charging along the first rock as if it's a race. "Arthur cycled this one," he calls over his shoulder. "Very cool, but also very foolish."

I follow Win, feeling like a bit of an idiot as the Lost Girls shuffle along behind us, with Stella taking notes on the ground. "We'll need to be quicker," she mutters. "Much quicker."

Win and I slip and slide on the pretend seaweed, which is realistic, but which also makes the Lost Girls crack up each time it happens. Rose drifts along with them, a bit like she's in a dream. She's been like this all morning.

"There's one problem," I say as I inch my way along the tightrope rock. "It's still not wet enough. When Win and I went along the Magic Road we were hit by waves on all sides. They made it hard to see and some of them were so big they nearly knocked us off our feet."

"They crashed down on our heads like a ton of water!" cries Win.

"Not a ton," I say. "More like a big bucketful."

After saying this, I suppose I shouldn't be surprised when a bucket of water is thrown in my face, followed by another and another. I drop to my knees on the tightrope rock—actually a plank of wood—and cling on. Hysterical giggles surround me. "There was a bit less water than that," I say as—smack—another one hits me and I fall to the ground.

Stella points at me. "If this was for real, Arthur Trout would be DEAD right now. His body would be speared on a

rock or being eaten by a shark somewhere in the Bottomless Ocean." She pauses for dramatic effect, then says, "Arthur, stop lounging around; everyone get back to the start. It's time for us to do this together, as a team . . . Team Roar!"

This makes Rose flinch with embarrassment, but she doesn't say anything. She knows Stella well enough not to risk offending her.

Stella organizes us into a line with me and Rose at the front—because we're the Masters of Roar—and Win in the middle.

"On your marks, get set, GET CROWKY!" Stella cries, and we're off.

It's a disaster. Three girls fall off the rocks straightaway, Win refuses to stay in line, and Rose simply goes through the motions, moving from obstacle to obstacle, but putting no real effort into it. When we reach the end—the big rock where Rose will call the dragons—half the Lost Girls have been left behind.

But we don't give up. We try again and again, and it does get better, but honestly I'm not sure if it's good enough. Tomorrow we'll need to cross the Magic Road in under an hour, in the dark, otherwise it will be a repeat of last time: Crowky will see us coming and then we'll be trapped. Or— and this is something I don't want to think about—we won't be quick enough and the tide will turn when we are only halfway across. . . .

"We need to rest now," says Stella, surveying Team Roar,

who are flopped all over the dojo, battered and bruised. "Try to get some sleep. We set off at dusk."

We stumble to our hammocks. The sun is bright, but it's shady under the trees and Win instantly falls asleep. I lie on my back and stare up at the leaves. I try to rest, but it's hard. My whole body is fizzing with hopes and worries, but more than anything I'm desperate to get going.

Not long now, Grandad, I think. *We're coming. I promise, we're coming.*

CHAPTER 34

It's Rose who shakes me awake. "Time to go," she says, her voice urgent.

I open my eyes and see a deep turquoise sky scattered with the first stars. I have this what's-going-on moment where I can't quite remember what's about to happen; I just know it's something out of the ordinary . . . Christmas Day? No. Going on vacation? No. Crossing a treacherous chain of rocks, flying a dragon through a small hole, and fighting my scarecrow nemesis? *Yes*, I think as I untangle myself from the hammock and stagger to my feet, *that's it.*

Rose thrusts a jam sandwich into my hands, saying, "Eat this, then we're off." She moves on to Win and drops his sandwich

on his stomach. "Wake up. We're going."

Win's eyes ping open. Instantly he rolls out of his hammock and into a leaping tiger kick. "BRING IT ON!" he cries, then he discovers his sandwich on the ground, dusts it off, and starts taking hungry bites.

We haven't all got Win's energy and it's a sleepy Team Roar who begin the long walk through the Tangled Forest. We break off the glowing buds to use as candles, and soon the twinkling line of lights, combined with worrying snuffles of strange creatures, wake me up.

The Lost Girls know every inch of the forest, and they lead us on a secret route that's far quicker than the one we took to find them. Stella also reassures us that the scarecrow army knows nothing about it. When we get to the top of the ravine we scramble down a zigzag path until we reach the river. There are no rapids here, and the girls pull canoes out from the branches of overhanging trees and we pile into them and paddle downstream.

It's totally dark now, but the crystals in the river still shine bright green. There are also fireflies darting around, attracted to the light from the buds. We move quickly down the river, our oars dipping in and out of the star-spangled water. It's magical, and I have to glance back at Rose to see what she thinks. But her face is a mask. She forces her oars through the water with grim determination and refuses to meet my eye.

We know when we reach the Bad Side.

First the fireflies go, then the buds on the trees, then our oars hit dead leaves. Soon the trees are bare skeletons stretching up into the cloudy night sky. There are no stars here.

Up ahead Stella steers the lead canoe toward the bank. We clamber out and Stella lets us have a short break. Just as some of the smallest Lost Girls are nodding off, she holds one of the glowing buds close to her face and whispers, "Now we walk. But remember, this is Crowky territory so total silence."

In single file we follow the path that takes us up into the mountains toward the Crow's Nest. Higher and higher we go. It's been two days since I did this journey with Win, and right now I can't quite believe we were brave enough, or stupid enough, to try to get there on our own.

Win's at the front of the line now because he knows how to find the Magic Tunnel. This means we take a couple of wrong turns and have to double back on ourselves, but soon I taste salt on the air and hear the crash of waves. We're getting close. I look up at the sky. I haven't got a clue what time it is. We've been traveling all night, but I'm sure the sky is a touch lighter now. We need to hurry up.

"We're here!" Win cries, earning him a chorus of shushes and a poke from Stella.

"Get rid of the buds," says Stella. "We can't let Crowky see us coming."

We throw the buds into a pile, then lift aside the curtain of ivy and scramble down the crack in the rock. We stumble over roots in our rush to get to the bottom and burst out on the ledge in the middle of the cliff. Win's bike has gone, presumably washed away by the tide, and ahead of us the Magic Road rises out of the Bottomless Ocean like a black snake. Far in the distance sits the towering hulk of the Crow's Nest.

CHAPTER 35

We huddle together as a wave smashes against the base of the cliff. The first rock on the Magic Road—the long thin one I cycled along—stretches in front of us. Only it looks even longer now. Every few seconds, water washes over it, hiding it from view.

"Look." I point at the sky, where a streak of gray is creeping into the blackness. "It's starting to get light. We can't wait for the water to go down any farther. We have to leave now." I turn to Rose. "Ready?" She nods. "Then let's go."

I walk forward and start to step along the rock. I try to go quickly, confidently, but it's so dark I'm not sure if my feet are going to land on solid rock or slip into the sea. "It's not so bad," I call over my shoulder. A wave washes over my toes and I freeze. "The next bit's easier."

Win comes behind me, although it's supposed to be Rose, then the Lost Girls follow. Rose and Stella are at the end. When Win and I reach the safety of the flat rock we don't stop to help the others across. We can't. We haven't got time.

"Now we jump!" Win calls. It's safe to shout here. No one could possibly hear us over the howling wind and growling sea. Either my eyes are adjusting, or it's getting lighter, because I find it easy to judge the distance between each rock and I get into a rhythm, running then jumping, scrambling to my feet and doing it again. Every now and then I pause to catch my breath and I watch the Lost Girls. They seem used to moving at night and looking out for each other. They jump between the rocks like cats, landing lightly, then springing up again. If someone slips, a hand grabs them. If someone falls back, a voice hisses, "Hurry up!"

We move closer to the Crow's Nest. I try not to look at it too often. Its round windows glow and flicker, and it's so big that down on the Magic Road I feel very small. Perhaps it's the Crow's Nest that makes us fall quiet, but by the time we reach the tunnel, no one is talking.

Win runs in first and we follow. The tunnel is dark and narrow, but I relax a bit. No one can fall in the sea here and it feels safe to be hidden from the Crow's Nest. But it is dark. When Win and I were here before, light came pouring in from each end of the tunnel, but now I have to feel my way after Win. Suddenly I bump into his back.

"Arthur, we've got a problem."

"What is it?"

"I'm standing in water."

I reach down and feel with my hands. He's right. His feet are surrounded by icy water.

"It's because we were quicker," I say. "The sea level hasn't dropped enough to empty the tunnel."

"What's going on?" Stella comes pushing past the girls who have bunched up behind me.

I explain what's happened, then for a moment we just stand there in the darkness listening to our breathing and the breaking waves. "We can't wait," I say. "You saw the sky. It's nearly dawn." Even now I can see gray light creeping into the mouth of the tunnel behind us. "If we stay here much longer, then we might come out in daylight. And what if the tide starts to turn before you get to the Crow's Nest?"

"And we can't go over this rock," Stella says. "It's too steep."

"So what do we do?" Rose's voice comes from the very end of the tunnel.

"We swim," says Stella, and before I can say anything she's slipped past me and plunged into the water.

One, two, three seconds pass. Drips fall from the roof of the tunnel.

"I don't like it in here," says a small voice near my elbow.

Suddenly there's an explosion of water and a black shape appears. "It's fine," says Stella. "You're only under the water for a moment, then you come out the other side. It's cold though. Get ready for that. Follow me, girls."

And with a splash she's gone.

For a second there's silence, then the Lost Girls scurry to follow their chief. One by one they push past me, throw themselves into the water, and disappear. I'm not sure if it's Stella's words or the fear of being left behind that makes them move so fast. Or maybe they're even tougher than I thought they were. One of them, Clara, I think, even shouts "HEAR ME ROAR!" before plunging in.

None of them hesitate. None of them come back, and soon it's just me, Win, and Rose left in the tunnel. "OK," says Win. "So . . . you reckon I just stick my head under and . . . swim?"

"I think so."

"See you on the other side," he says, then he ducks down and the inky water swallows him up. With one kick of his sneakers he's gone.

"Do you want to go next?" I ask Rose. I see her shake her head. "What? So . . . you'll follow me?"

"No." Her voice is quiet. "I can't do it."

I hadn't expected this, but then I realize just how dark the tunnel is. Rose hates the dark. Swimming through a pitch-black tunnel is hard for me, but it must be terrifying for her. I decide to try the technique Win used on me.

"Of course you can do it, Rose. You're a Master of Roar. Plus, you're not scared of anything!"

She laughs bitterly. "I'm scared of loads of things."

"Like what?"

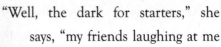

"Well, the dark for starters," she says, "my friends laughing at me because I've still got a massive collection of dragons—actually, being laughed at full stop—my friends not wanting to hang out with me anymore. That's four things off the top of my head, Arthur."

I think back to the names Rose wrote down when our classes were mixed up. Maybe she didn't put me down because she was scared about what would happen if she wasn't with her friends.

"I'm no hero and I'm no Master of Roar," Rose says, sinking to the floor of the tunnel. Now she's just a ball in the darkness. "In fact, I'm no better than Crowky because I've been pulling this place apart."

I sit next to her. Hard rock presses into my back and Rose's shoulder trembles next to mine. "Listen, Rose, I don't care that you gave away our dragons—even though they were very cool—or the fact that I embarrass you all the time, and you frequently call me a loser—"

"I call you a doofus too."

"And sometimes a dorkasaurus—my point is, I get why you do those things because I'm scared of loads of stuff too.

What I care about is that you're my twin—my only twin—and not only can you speak three made-up languages—Mermish, Moonlight Stallion, and Dragon—you made this world with me. You are my sister, and you are a Master of Roar, and nothing can ever, *ever* change that." And then I do something incredibly brave. In fact, it's possibly the bravest thing I've done in my life. I put my arm around Rose's shoulders and I give them a squeeze.

For a few seconds we just sit like that, squashed in the cold, dark tunnel.

"Hey," I say, breaking the silence, "aren't you going to call me a loser? Because that was probably the most loserish thing I've ever done in my life."

"You weren't being a loser," Rose says, resting her head on my shoulder. "You were being kind."

Rose and I sit like this for about two minutes. I don't think either of us enjoy it exactly, but it feels grown-up, and grown-up is what we need to feel right now.

Then I pull Rose to her feet. "Now swim through that tunnel, Rose Trout, Master of Roar."

And she does. She takes a deep breath, and she's gone with barely a splash. I take one last glance behind me, then follow her into the icy water.

CHAPTER 36

Two hands grab hold of me and pull me out of the water. It's Win. "What took you so long? You've been ages!"

I don't answer, I just start running. We burst out of the tunnel and immediately I notice how light it's gotten. It's still gloomy, but now I can clearly see the crooked towers of the Crow's Nest and its tall wooden doors. We can't waste a second. Up ahead the Lost Girls have carried on jumping along the rocks with Stella at the lead. Rose is catching up with them. She clears the Big Leap with ease. She's not drifting now. She's on fire.

Win and I follow, and we run flat out along the Magic Road. We pass the rock where the scarecrows attacked us and keep going. We're going faster than in any of our training sessions. We're going faster than I thought possible.

The Lost Girls reach the large rock where we're going to summon the dragons and Rose leaps on after them.

"Hurry up!" Stella calls back to us, before a wave crashes over the rock, hiding them from view.

Win and I jump onto the last rock and run to join the girls, who are bunched together in the middle. I feel exposed on this wide rock with the Crow's Nest so near. Plus the crack runs right through it, almost splitting it in two.

"Quick," I say to Rose. "Call them."

Rose puts two fingers to her lips and whistles. The sound is immediately drowned out by the waves.

"Will that really work?" asks Stella.

"I was there when they hatched," says Rose firmly. "My voice was the first they heard. They *will* hear me."

I look up. Rose sounds different. Rose sounds like a Master of Roar. And she's standing like one too: on her own at the edge of the group, back straight, staring toward land and watching for her dragons.

The rest of us haven't quite got her confidence. We huddle up, shifting uncomfortably and willing the dragons to appear. Suddenly a lone crow circles above us. It caws, its beady eyes watching us closely. Win meets my eye. Like me, he's wondering if this is just a curious bird or one of Crowky's spies.

"There!" Rose points at two dots far away in the sky. "The dragons are coming."

The sight of the two huge dragons approaching is a relief, but it makes me feel more exposed. Perhaps the others feel it too, because we gather even closer together. "This is it," says Stella. "We need to get going, tackle the last bit of the Magic Road, but first we do our war cry. Girls?"

The Lost Girls know what to do. "Lost Girls! Lost Girls! LOST GIRLS! LOST GIRLS!" they chant, their voices rising above the sound of the sea. At the same time they stomp their feet up and down, and I can't help glancing nervously at the crack that cuts across the rock.

With a final yell of "LOST GIRLS!" they fall silent.

Stella turns to me and Rose. "Go on. Your turn. Say your thing."

Despite her newfound confidence, Rose develops a sudden fascination with her feet so I'm forced to lift my fist in the air and shout, "Hear me roar!" I sound totally pathetic.

"Rooooaaaar!" goes Win, clawing at the air with his hands. He doesn't help.

"*That's it?*" Stella yells. "We're about to fight the scarecrow army for *your* grandad and that's all the encouragement you can give us?"

"I know," I say, my teeth chattering from the cold, "and we're massively grateful, but look at the sky. It's almost morning. You need to get going!"

Stella opens her mouth, but before she can speak Rose steps forward. "I have got something to say, but it's not the 'hear me roar' thing." Everyone turns to look at her and she raises her voice so she can be heard over the wind and waves. "I just wanted to tell you that our grandad is a man worth saving."

"Go on," says Stella. "We're listening."

"When I was little I got everyone to come and watch me fly down the stairs. Only it turned out I was just jumping with my eyes shut and flapping my arms. Grandad said that the only reason it didn't work was because I didn't have wings." She pauses and takes a deep breath. "So he made me a pair out of real feathers; they were beautiful and soft, and when we went to the beach and I put them on and ran across the sand Grandad said he saw me fly. He said I was magnificent."

The Lost Girls are listening to Rose with wide eyes, their hair sticking in wet strands to their cheeks. "Flying was the second best thing that's ever happened to me," says Rose, "and it was Grandad who made it happen, just by believing in me. He's an amazing person and he doesn't deserve to be locked up by Crowky." Rose looks in turn at Win, Stella, and the Lost Girls. "I just wanted to say that I know we can do this . . . because I believe in you." Her eyes settle on me. "I believe in all of you."

For a moment there is silence.

Then the rock beneath our feet starts to shake, and a groaning comes from the sea as the water starts to froth and foam.

"What's going on?" says Stella.

"Look!" I point at the crack in the rock. Stones and earth are bubbling up inside it as the two sides tremble and shift up and down. We're thrown from side to side, and I'm about to turn and make a dash for the next rock when I realize that

the crack isn't getting bigger. It's getting smaller, and in front of our eyes it seals shut like a zipper.

"Imaginary," Win whispers.

I sigh with relief. "Totally!" Then I glance back along the Magic Road and what I see makes my blood run cold. Rock by rock, the Magic Road is disappearing into the sea.

Rose sees it too. "What's happening?"

"I think you mended Roar," I say.

"And now that the crack's gone, the sea is coming back!" cries Win.

Rose turns to Stella. "You've got to get to the castle! Quickly!"

Stella doesn't hesitate. She shouts an instruction and the Lost Girls jump onto the next rock and run forward.

"Do you think they'll make it?" says Win.

"Will *we* make it?" I say, my eyes flicking from the approaching dragons to the vanishing rocks. A huge wave is sweeping toward us now, a tsunami, and it's swallowing up the Magic Road.

Rose whistles again, but I don't think the dragons can go any faster. They're diving toward us, wings back, snouts down, their talons grazing the sea. They're racing the wave, overtaking it.

We stand at the edge of the rock, trying to give the dragons as much room as possible to land. Pickle comes first, skidding to a stop by our feet. Rose leaps forward and scrambles onto his back. "Gobo, Gobo!" she cries, and they're off, clearing the rock seconds before Vlad crashes down.

Then the wave hits.

I throw myself at Vlad's side and my fingers find a spike as the water sucks at my legs. Win grabs hold of a spike too. "GOBO!" I cry, and Vlad rises up in the air, plucking us out of the sea. As he chases after Pickle we heave our soaking bodies onto his back.

I look down. The Lost Girls have almost reached the Crow's Nest, but the wave is catching up with them. Stella is at the front. She takes a giant leap, landing on the rock that forms the base of the castle. As the rest of the Lost Girls pile after her, the castle's doors swing open. A scarecrow appears in the doorway, then another, and another, and then they're pouring out, charging straight toward the Lost Girls. Crows follow them, bursting out of the door and the windows of the castle and diving after the scarecrows.

There is one girl left on the Magic Road. She jumps, her braids flying behind her.

Vlad sweeps around the side of the Crow's Nest and the Lost Girls are hidden from view.

CHAPTER 37

Rose takes Pickle out to sea, and we follow.

The sight of the last girl disappearing is seared into my mind. My instinct tells me to go back, but I tell myself that the Lost Girls look after each other and Stella wouldn't lose one of her girls.

Right now it's Grandad who needs me.

"Fobastober!" I shout. But I barely need to instruct Vlad. He's flying so fast that his nose almost brushes Pickle's tail. Ahead, Pickle starts to turn, rising up at the same time. I know what Rose is doing. She wants Pickle in the perfect position, ready for the dive toward the cave.

"Can you see it?" calls Win.

I scan the rocky cliff below the castle, looking for the entrance to the cave, but before I've even spotted it Rose yells, "Foborwobard!" and commands Pickle to dive straight toward the cliff face. Vlad follows. At first I think we're heading toward sheer rock, then I see a black opening, more a crack than a cave. "Dobive, DOBIVE!" cries Rose, and the dragons throw back their wings as they shoot toward the crack.

Win grabs my shoulder. "Arthur . . . I've got a bad feeling about this!"

My hands tighten on the spike. The air screams past me. Like Win I can't quite believe this is going to work. The cave looks tiny, and the dragons' wings are so wide. We can't enter the cave head-on, but if we tilt, we might make it.

"I'm shutting my eyes!" Win cries. "I can't watch."

I can't shut my eyes. Even if we wanted to, we're going too fast to turn the dragons now, and Rose is already urging Pickle farther and farther over until his wing is pointing toward the sea. "Lobeft . . . Lobeft." I press my leg into Vlad's neck. I'm not sure if I need to. Already he's started to turn. I squeeze my hands tighter around the spike and Win clings on to me. *This is it*, I think as the cliff looms up to meet us. *This is it.*

With a cry Pickle soars inside the cave. At the last second he throws out a ball of fire and I have no choice but to fly Vlad straight into the flames. I shut my eyes and brace my body, preparing for anything. I feel burning flames brush over my skin followed by blackness and then blissfully cool air.

I open my eyes. "Win, we're in the cave!" My voice echoes in the darkness. "We did it! WE DID IT!"

Vlad roars, lighting up the tunnel, and I see that we're still flying over the sea. Ahead Pickle is preparing to land next to the huge bulk of the *Raven*.

"Vlad, slobow dobown!" I shout as we shoot past the *Raven*. Vlad pulls in his wings and stretches out his talons.

"Can I look?" Win yells.

"Not yet!"

Vlad lands with a crash, sending me and Win tumbling to the rocky ground.

Rose pulls us up. "Can you believe it?" Her whispered voice echoes around us. "We actually did it!"

I look up. The *Raven* towers over us. The ship is tall and narrow, the perfect shape to slip in and out of the cave. She sways gently in her mooring, her ancient timbers creaking as waves lap against her side. Water drips and the cave is filled with the *Raven*'s smell of tar and tanned leather.

Finally we're inside the Crow's Nest . . .

"We have to move fast." I half run toward the back of the cave and Rose follows. "Even if Crowky didn't see us on the dragons he'll know that the attack has got something to do with us. He's probably searching the castle right now!"

Win calls after us, "Do I have to stay here?"

"Yes, we agreed," says Rose. "You have to look after the dragons. They're our getaway vehicles."

"But why me?" Win stares back at the *Raven*. "That thing gives me the creeps."

The ship's sails are down, but there's still something chilling about the way the oily leather ripples in the breeze, like she's a sleeping creature waiting to spring into life. We've never seen the *Raven* like this, inside the Crow's Nest.

"It's a boat," I say. "That's all.... She just looks menacing."

Win nods, then runs over and pulls us to him. "Be careful. I want to see three of you coming back, not two . . . and definitely not zero."

It isn't like Win to be so worried. But I understand. This place feels rotten. Even the dragons look unsettled. They're pacing the flat rock, deep growls rumbling inside them and smoke seeping from their mouths.

"We will," I say, then we wriggle from his arms and run toward a wide stone staircase. It's lit by flickering torches and as we go up, taking the stairs two at a time, our long shadows dance along the wall.

"Don't let those dragons go anywhere!" Rose calls back, then we turn a corner and we're on our own in the Crow's Nest.

CHAPTER 38

The staircase turns in a wide spiral.

Each time we go around a corner we're expecting to come face-to-face with a scarecrow, but no one is there. We don't stop to think about what's happened to Crowky's guards, we just take our chance and run as fast as we can.

The walls are splattered with crusty white goo, feathers, and dirty straw. The muck spreads under our feet, muffling our footsteps. We climb higher. The air gets colder. Soon I can see puffs of mist each time I breathe out. At the top of the staircase we burst out into a round, dimly lit chamber with passageways leading in all directions. It's vast, like a cathedral, and it's filthy and smells unmistakably of bird.

Rose looks dismayed. "Which way do we go? We need a map!" Her voice echoes around us.

A *map* . . . I feel in my back pocket. "We've got one!"

"That can't help us," says Rose. "We've never been here so we won't have put these tunnels on the map."

But I'm already unfolding it, remembering something odd

that I saw in Grandad's attic. I hold the map up to the light of a torch.

"There." I point at the picture of the Crow's Nest. Just below it is a series of squiggly lines. My eyes flicked over it in the attic, but now I see that these aren't random scribbles at all: they show the tunnels we're standing in.

"I don't believe it," whispers Rose. "Mitch must have told us about this. She's the only one who came in here." With her finger she traces the narrow entrance of the sea cave to a tiny set of stairs. "We're here." She points at a spot where six passageways lead off in different directions.

"And look." I've found a circular chamber with *dungun* written above it. I trace backward from the dungeon to the point on the map where we are standing, like I'm doing a maze in a puzzle book.

"It's that one." Rose nods toward the opening directly in front of us.

I stuff the map back into my pocket—secretly thanking Mitch, wherever she is—and we run into the wide passageway. Like the stairs, it curves around and around and seems to rise upward. The walls are coated in the same feathery muck and every now and then my feet slip in something, but we keep going until we turn a corner and enormous pale moths with milky eyes flit around our heads.

"Seriously creepy," whispers Rose.

I nod, batting the moths away. I can't shake the feeling that something about this feels wrong, and it's not just the giant moths. It's too quiet down here. Would Crowky really leave his dungeons unguarded? The silence makes me jumpy and I start to see movements in the shadows and imagine scarecrows creeping up behind us, or worse, Crowky.

"Come on," says Rose, pulling me away.

The passageway straightens out into a gloomy tunnel with thick wooden doors set into the walls. Each door has a rusting lock and sliding hatch. They look like cells and strange sounds drift from behind some of them: flutters and stamps and scratches. Rose and I look at each other. Grandad could be behind any one of these doors.

Trying to make as little noise as possible, I slide back  the hatch on the first door and peer inside. Cool air brushes against my face and in the gloom I see cages lining the walls. At first I think they're empty, but then shapes creep forward and eyes blink back at me. Two wings emerge from a cage and curl around the bars like fingers. I've never seen creatures like this in Roar. They're like crows but far bigger.

"There are cages," I whisper to Rose, "lots of them, with birds inside. At least, I think they're birds."

I step back so she can see.

She shakes her head. "Whatever they are, they shouldn't be locked up in this disgusting place. We have to let them out!"

She goes to try the door handle, but I pull her back. "No. We don't know what they'll do. We can't do anything that might stop us from finding Grandad!"

Reluctantly Rose nods, and we continue down the passageway, peering into each chamber as we go. We don't find Grandad, but we see a lot of unsettling things: a workshop with a collection of half-made scarecrows propped against the walls and sack heads arranged on a shelf; a laboratory with potions bubbling in flasks; there's even a room filled with dusty-looking creatures—a mermaid with peeling scales, a unicorn resting against the wall, a whole line of tiny fuzzies.

"I think these are all things that got stuffed and stayed stuffed," I say, then we check carefully to make sure Grandad isn't propped up in there with them.

It all feels horribly unfamiliar. Until now, no matter how strange everything has been in Roar, Rose or I have had a connection to it. Even Crowky is made up of things I hate. But these cells have nothing to do with us. We're in Crowky's world now.

The last cell is different. It contains nothing but cardboard boxes.

I know these boxes are important, but I can't remember why. Just the sight of them sends a shiver slipping down my spine. I slam the hatch shut.

"He's not in there," I say. "Let's go."

But Rose isn't listening. She's staring at something scratched into the wall of the tunnel. "Pictures," she says, and in the dim light I see them too: a jumble of images and symbols scored over and over again on the walls.

Rose seems hypnotized by them. "Come on." I pull her away. "We've wasted enough time here already."

We run away from the cells down the passageway. It's even wider here, and colder. A lone moth brushes against my face.

"Look!" says Rose.

Up ahead is a huge doorway. It rises to the ceiling and has a shape burned into it: two upturned wings that seem to form a smile. We rush forward and Rose has to use both hands to pull back the bolt. Then we push against the door. It won't budge, so we throw all our weight against it, again and again. Until it bursts open with a deafening squeal.

And there, standing on a stone platform, his arms outstretched, his eyes staring into space and his ankles clamped in chains, is Grandad.

CHAPTER 39

"Grandad!" We tear across the chamber and clamber onto the platform.

Grandad doesn't move—he can't move—and as I throw my arms around him I realize how cold he is. It's like I'm hugging a scarecrow dressed in Grandad's clothes. I even hear the crackle of something that might be straw when I squeeze him tight.

"We're here, Grandad." Rose's voice trembles as she tugs at his cardigan. "We've come to take you home."

I cup my hands around his face. His beard feels spiky. His cheeks are cold as stone. His cardigan smells faintly of coffee. "Grandad . . . can you hear us?"

"We've come to take you home," Rose repeats, her arms wrapped tightly around his waist. "Please wake up!" Her voice is desperate. It's how I feel too. His dry, vacant eyes and still chest tell me that we're too late. We were stupid to think there were rules about how long we had to get to Grandad. Crowky doesn't have rules. Everything about him and his castle is chaotic and messed up.

But I'm not ready to give up and suddenly I have to have Grandad back. Rose must feel this too because we both start rubbing his cheeks and his hands, and calling out to him.

The side of my face is pressed against him when a deep wheeze comes rattling out of his parted lips. It sounds terrible, but it's a sign of life and when we hear another one, and then another, we're so relieved we laugh.

His eyes squeeze shut. "Arthur, Rose . . . ?" His voice is a hoarse whisper.

"Grandad!" we cry.

One of his arms flops down and I grab hold of it. Warm fingers curl around mine. Then his other arm drops and he collapses heavily to the ground. He pulls us into a weak hug. I hold him tight until I realize that he's struggling to suck in air.

"Here." I find his inhaler and he takes it from me and sticks it in his mouth. He's supposed to shake it. He's supposed to take slow, deep breaths. But his fumbling fingers pump the canister again and again, and he sucks in the medicine until I pull it away from him. "Give it a chance to work," I say, "and you need to save some."

He nods, then half opens his eyes and rests his head against the wall. Squeezing our hands, he breathes like he's greedy for air, until gradually his breathing slows, then falls into a regular rhythm. Rose finds a dirty blanket on the floor and drapes it over his shoulders.

Eventually he's strong enough to look from Rose to me. Then we see the flicker of a smile. "Looks like Roar does still exist, Arthur."

"I'm sorry." It's all I can think to say.

His eyes dart around the chamber. He swallows, then licks his dry lips. "Nothing to be sorry about. . . . Look at this place."

I take in the cavernous room that Grandad's imprisoned in. It's round and looks like a large, empty theater. It has a domed ceiling and stone walls that are blackened, like they've been scorched by flame, although it's bitterly cold in here. Above us, circling the whole dungeon, is a gallery.

"The scarecrow usually appears up there," Grandad says, nodding toward the gallery. "Sometimes he says nasty things, but usually he just stares at me, then goes away again." His voice sounds dry and rusty and I wish I had some water to give him.

"This place is horrible," says Rose.

Grandad manages to shake his head. "It's incredible, Rose. Cold, yes, and dirty, but quite incredible and I'm alive, aren't I? That thing he did to me, squeezing me, it was painful and frightening, but it actually stopped my wheezing." He smiles, but it doesn't convince me or Rose. It's a weary smile that doesn't reach his eyes. "But he *does not* like you two. You need to get out of here!"

"We're not leaving without you," I say. "Right now an army of girls is attacking the castle. This is our chance to get you out of here!"

Grandad lifts up one foot and rattles his chains. "Better get rid of these then."

"Definitely," I say, picking up one of the chains and following it to where it loops through the ring in the wall. "We need a tool. Something to smash it."

Rose and I jump off the platform and explore the chamber, trying to find something, anything we can use. But except for the torches and a few bits of straw and the blanket, the chamber is empty. "Arthur, you stay here," says Rose. "I'll look in the cells." Then she runs out of the room.

"Come here, Arthur." Grandad pats the floor next to him. "Share my blanket." I climb back onto the platform and sit next to him. Grandad throws his dirty blanket over my legs. "It's not very nice," he says. "I think it might have come from Crowky's bed. Or does he sleep in a nest?"

"I don't know. I don't know much about him at all. I'm just starting to realize that. Roar has gotten a bit . . . wild."

"It's magnificent." The effort of saying this last word makes him rest his head back against the wall, close his eyes, and take several deep, wheezing breaths. He has two more blasts on the inhaler. "Bliss . . ."

For a moment we just sit there and listen to Grandad's breathing as it slows down. Then I decide to ask him something that I've been thinking about ever since I arrived in Roar.

"Grandad . . . how come you knew this place was real? I thought you were trying to get me to play. But you weren't, were you?"

Eyes still closed, he shakes his head.

"And up in the attic, when I said I'd been bitten by a real dragon, you didn't even blink."

He turns to me and opens his eyes. "Arthur, I believed that you'd been bitten by a dragon because *I've* been bitten by a dragon too." He pulls up his shorts, and there, just above his knee, is a thin scar. "When I was a little boy I found this . . . magical place, just like you found Roar. I visited it. I played in it. I've had a long time to think about it and I wonder if every child has a world like this, only not all of them are lucky enough to find it."

"But if you're right, everyone would be talking about it. It would be on the news and the internet."

"Arthur, if you listen you'll realize everyone *is* talking about it! Ask someone about the best game they ever played, and you will see it in their eyes. They go back there, just for a moment, as they remember a magical time. They don't know they're describing something real. It's become nothing more than a game to them." As Grandad talks he seems to get stronger. "Maybe these worlds are all over the internet: ghosts, trolls, fairies, the Loch Ness Monster! Where do they all come from?"

"A world like this. . . ."

"Exactly!"

I frown. "How come you can still remember your world? I'm eleven and I'd almost forgotten Roar."

"I can still remember my world because I have never stopped visiting it!" Grandad's eyes light up, as if he's been longing to tell me this.

"But . . . where is it?"

"It's at the back of the jam cupboard in the cellar."

I laugh, then stop when I realize that he's serious. I picture the cupboard in the corner of Grandad's cellar. It came from Mauritius and I've always liked it because it looks like it might have been kept in a pirate captain's room, all carved wood and flowers made out of shells. It's tucked between the chest freezer and the coal store, and full of twenty-year-old pickled onions and dusty bottles of pineapple jam.

"Do you still go there?"

Grandad nods. "Sometimes. It's quite a squeeze these days. My knees aren't so good and while I've gotten bigger the jam cupboard has stayed the same size. I've often wondered why it's never gone away. Perhaps it's because I've never grown up, not properly."

"What's it like?"

He laughs. "Incredible. I've always wanted to tell you about it. . . . There are no scarecrows, thank goodness, and it's very watery: floating cities and forests, and ships that can lift off the water and sail through the sky. There's this palace of ice that drifts on a cloud. That's where my dragons live. I've been very lucky to have it."

Something about how Grandad says this, as if he's almost given up on seeing his world again, makes me jump to my feet. "Grandad, we're getting you out of here." I pull at the chains clamped around his ankles, trying to think of some way we can wrench them apart. "I promise. Right now the Lost Girls are fighting Crowky and his scarecrows, and we've got dragons waiting for us. As soon as we get these chains off, we can take you home!"

Rose runs back into the chamber and I see that her hands are empty. "I'm sorry," she says. "All the doors were locked."

In a panic I blurt out, "I'll get Win."

Rose looks amazed. "*Win? What can he do?*"

"Maybe he could use his magic to blow the chains apart."

"Win couldn't use his magic to blow a daisy chain apart. . . . But the dragons might be able to melt them."

I try to imagine the dragons finding us, pushing their way through all the passageways. Would it be possible? We have to try. "I'll fetch them," I say, jumping down from the platform.

I'm running toward the door when it slams shut in

my face. The bang echoes around the chamber. I grab the handle and push as hard as I can. At first I think it's jammed shut, but then I realize the door is locked, and that means someone has locked it. "Win!" I yell, banging my hands down on thick wood. "*WIN!*"

With a rusty scrape the hatch in the middle of the door slides open. Taking a deep breath, I step closer and look into the dark tunnel. And that's when I hear a ruffle of feathers, and a scratchy voice hisses, "I've got you now, Arthur Trout!"

CHAPTER 40

Crowky steps out of the shadows and stares at me. His hair is sticking up even more wildly and he's still wearing Grandad's T-shirt, only now it's ripped and grubby. Suddenly he grins and his smile is so wide that a couple of stitches pop open and some straw floats to the ground. "*Amazing.* . . . Roar's mighty masters, Rose and Arthur Trout, simply walk into their very own dungeon!"

"Let us out," I say, standing as close to the bars as I dare.

Rose appears at my side. "Let us take our grandad and go home," she says. "You never have to see us again!"

Crowky's eyes grow wide. "Oh, but I *want* to see you, Rose. I want to see you all the time."

"What do you mean?"

His stick fingers grip the bars. "I worked something out that everyone else was too stupid to notice." He pushes his sack face against the bars. "We *need* you. You always disappeared for a while, went to Home, or whatever that place is called, but then you'd turn up again like a bad smell."

This is too much for Rose. "*We're* the bad smell?"

Crowky puts a finger to his lips. "*Shhh.* Then, one day, you just stopped coming. Months, then years passed with no sign of Arthur or Rose. At first it was marvelous. The mischief I caused!" His face lights up before twisting into a scowl. "But strange things started to happen. First, there were the earth wobbles, then holes appeared in the most inconvenient places and things started to disappear. The unicorns were the first to go. I couldn't care less about them, but when *these* stopped working . . ." He hunches his shoulders, letting his wings unfold until they're brushing the sides of the tunnel. They beat once, twice, sending a single feather floating through the bars, "I was furious. And all because of *you*. But I wasn't going to sit in my castle, moldering. I built my army. I made spies that could fly for me. But what good were they if Roar was splitting in two? Although it pains me to say it, without Arthur and Rose Trout, Roar falls apart. Literally!"

"How do you know all those things happened because of us?"

My words must sound hollow because Crowky throws his head back and cackles. "It has *everything* to do with you! When you turned up at the Crow's Nest I flew for the first time in years!"

Rose shakes her head in disbelief. "So . . . what? You're just going to keep us here?"

He smiles and nods. "I spent hours in that tunnel waiting for you to come back. Then, finally, that old man came

through and when he started calling out for Arthur . . . Well.
I knew it was only a matter of time until you came looking
for him. Yes, I'm keeping you here, Rose Trout. I'm keeping
you here *forever*."

Crowky says these words with such relish that dread sweeps through me. Will we be a case on the news: two children and their grandad who vanish during their summer vacation?

Rose must feel this too because she grabs hold of my arm. "You can't do that!"

"Oh yes I can. But I won't just keep you here, Rose, I'll *terrify* you here! Down in my dungeon you won't be feeling happy thoughts. I'll keep you scared. I'll keep you wondering what wicked thing I'm going to do next."

"But . . . why?" asks Rose.

He presses his face into the bars. "For FUN, Rose, because it's what I do!"

I grab Rose's hand and she squeezes my fingers tight.

"I've enjoyed waiting for you to find your way here," Crowky continues. "I've imagined every little moment of panic you've had, every scare, every pinprick of fear . . . and it felt GOOD!"

This is too much for Rose. "Let us out! You can't keep us here!"

"Yes I can, Rose, but I won't keep the old man. I have no use for him now that he's lured you to me . . . well, except as food." With a grin Crowky grabs a lever set in the wall and yanks it down.

A groaning, clanking sound throbs through the chamber and the stones under our feet start to tremble. Then the whole floor begins to slide back, taking us with it.

"Rose . . . Arthur," says Grandad, "what's going on?"

When we turn around we understand. The floor of the chamber is disappearing into the walls and a gaping hole is opening up. If the floor doesn't stop moving soon Grandad's going to be stranded! Without stopping to think, I run forward and jump.

I land on the edge of the platform with my legs hanging down in the hole. I quickly pull myself up and rush over to Grandad. With a sudden thud the floor stops moving. Now a great pit lies between us and Rose. She stares at us through the smoke drifting out of the pit. "What did you do that for?" she cries.

That's when I realize I've left her all on her own.

"Yes, *Arthur*, that was a very foolish thing to do!" Crowky's voice echoes from somewhere above. He must have left the doorway because he's now staring down at us from the gallery. He paces up and down, his wings fluttering with fidgety excitement. "I'm not going to let your pathetic heroics ruin my plan. I've been looking forward to this for such a long time."

Grandad tugs on my sleeve. "What's in that hole, Arthur?"

I crawl to the edge of the platform and peer over. A disgusting smell drifts out of the pit: a mixture of meat, sulfur, and something that reminds me of the reptile house at the zoo. Fear prickles over my skin as if my body can sense danger, and then, far down in the pit, I see movement.

Something is crawling toward me.

"What *is* that?" I whisper.

Crowky leans over the wall of the gallery and cackles. "Someone very, very hungry, but don't worry. She only eats food from her special feeding area. . . . Oh no! Your grandad appears to be chained to her special feeding area!"

The huge, gnarly creature creeps higher up the wall and into the dim light. She has red eyes and thick, cracked skin. Black smoke seeps from her nostrils and her teeth glint in the darkness.

I gasp. "Bad Dragon . . . !"

As if in reply, Bad Dragon opens her jaws in a deadly grin and breathes out. Flames race up the wall of the pit, sending me scurrying back toward Grandad. He pulls me to him, and we press our backs against the wall as the flames lick our feet.

"Arthur," he says, "is it my imagination or is it getting hot in here?"

CHAPTER 41

Rose puts two fingers to her lips and whistles. She does it again and again.

"No one can hear you," calls Crowky in a singsong voice, just as Bad Dragon's snout appears over the side of the pit, followed by her enormous craggy head. She sniffs the air curiously.

Rose whistles again and again, but I can't believe the sound can travel through all the twisting stone passageways back to the sea cave.

"Sit back and enjoy the show, Rose," says Crowky. "Although I should warn you, Bad Dragon is a very messy eater. Arthur, you might like to step to one side. We don't want her thinking you're dessert."

"Arthur"—Grandad tugs on my sleeve—"am I right in thinking a dragon of the 'bad variety' is crawling out of that hole with the intention of eating me?" His voice is surprisingly calm, even though the flames billowing from the pit are making him drip with sweat.

"Yes . . . that's pretty much it. We're sitting in her feeding area."

He tries to push me away. "Then get away from me!"

I shake my head and watch as Bad Dragon starts to heave herself out of the hole. "Rose!" I shout. "Can't you stop her? You used to be able to make her roll over with one click of your fingers!"

"Gobood gobirl," says Rose gently. "Cobome tobo Mobummy . . ."

Bad Dragon twists her head toward Rose and stares at her, eyes narrowed. Suddenly her jaws snap open and she sends out a blast of fire that makes Rose stagger back.

Crowky laughs. "You're just a tasty morsel to her now. No different frrom any of the other snacks I toss down there."

Bad Dragon's claws grip the edge of the pit and her eyes slide back toward her feeding ledge and me and Grandad.

And that's when I hear a distant *thud, thud, thud* of pounding feet. Bad Dragon hears them too, and tilts her head slightly. The thuds get louder, and there's a smashing sound as if something is bashing against the walls of the tunnel. Then there's a huge crash as something slams into the door. The thick wood splinters, but it doesn't break. Up on the gallery, Crowky snarls with annoyance.

Suddenly Win's face appears at the bars. His eyes widen in horror. "Guys . . . I don't know if you've noticed, but Bad Dragon is, like, right there!" Behind him I can see two large bodies, one red and the other blue. It's Pickle and Vlad!

Rose runs to the door. "Help me get Pickle and Vlad to breathe fire on the door. We need to burn it down. Arthur, you distract Bad Dragon!"

"What? How do I do that?"

"Think of something!" Rose starts issuing a series of Obby Dobby commands to Pickle and Vlad.

All Bad Dragon's greedy attention is focused on Grandad. "Oi!" I shout, waving my arms around and moving away from Grandad. "Over here, you big ugly beast!"

Bad Dragon ignores me and snarls at Grandad, singeing the edge of his blanket. I feel in my pockets and pull out the first thing I find: Grandad's carrot key ring. I hurl it at Bad Dragon's head, but with one puff of fire she turns it to ash. At least I've got her attention. Her eyes narrow again and she stares hard at me.

"Arthur, do something *quickly!*" cries Rose.

So I start randomly moving my arms and legs around and yelling and shouting. Before I know what I'm doing, I'm dancing. I do the whip and the nae nae and the floss, and because Bad Dragon is still staring at me, mesmerized, I don't stop. I dance like Dad, flapping my arms like a chicken and jerking my knees up and down.

"WHOOP!" goes Grandad. "Here comes the beat, Arthur!" Then he starts making strange sounds and I realize he's beatboxing.

"What *ARE* you doing?" sneers Crowky.

"What does it look like I'm doing?" I shout. "I'm

DANCING." I attempt to moonwalk, fall over, and Bad Dragon incinerates my sneakers. I yelp and clutch at my burning heels while Bad Dragon turns away to sniff out Grandad, drawn to his squeaky noises.

"Be quiet, Grandad!" I yell, and Crowky hangs over the wall of the gallery, shaking with laughter.

"Just a few more seconds . . . !" shouts Rose. She's pressed against the wall of the chamber, keeping back from the barrage of flames that's hammering the door. Suddenly Bad Dragon lunges, snatching up Grandad's blanket and tossing it into the pit.

"BLIMEY!" cries Grandad.

I cup my hands around my mouth. "Win, CHUCK ME YOUR WAND!"

From the hatch in the door Win's wand comes flying through the air. I make a grab for it, but it doesn't quite reach me and lands on Bad Dragon's back. Before I can take a step toward it, there's a bang and a flash of pink stars and suddenly Win is sitting on Bad Dragon, his mouth hanging open.

"I did it! I did an AWESOME spell. Did everyone see? I just said the first thing that came into my head, and I flew or disappeared or dissolved or something!"

Bad Dragon whips her head around to see who's making all the noise and that's when Win realizes where he is.

"ARRRGHHHH! I'm sitting on Bad Dragon! Help me, Arthur, HELP ME!"

With one twitch of her body Bad Dragon tosses Win to the ground.

I drag him back next to Grandad, then the three of us sit squashed together as Bad Dragon leans over us. Her black tongue starts flicking around our faces like she's tasting us one by one. I shut my eyes as she turns her attention to me. The heat is almost unbearable and the stench of sulfur makes me dizzy. Just when I think I can't stand it any longer, there's an almighty crash and I open my eyes to see Pickle forcing his way through the burning door with Vlad close behind him.

Bad Dragon must think they're after her food because her spikes ripple and she breathes a blast of flames right at them. Vlad responds with his own barrage of fire and then the chamber becomes an inferno.

Grandad, Win, and I cover our heads to protect ourselves from the sparks that rain down. While Vlad and Bad Dragon battle with fire, Rose guides Pickle closer to the edge of the pit. "Win, Arthur, move!" she calls, before instructing Pickle to "Mobelt thobose chobains!"

All it takes is one carefully directed flame and Grandad's chains turn into molten liquid.

"Ow, ow, ow!" he cries, rubbing his ankles, but Win and I are already pulling him up. Above us Crowky screams with rage. He can't move. He's trapped on the gallery by the flames.

Rose leads Pickle even closer to the edge of the pit and he stretches his neck toward us. He can't quite reach, but Win is still able to jump across onto his huge head. Next it's Grandad's turn. I can hardly bear to look as he leaps blindly toward the dragon's head, but Win grabs hold of his cardigan and hauls him to safety. I follow, then the three of us slip and slide across Pickle's neck until we're squashed together on his back.

Rose helps me down, but waves Win back. "Stay on Pickle," she says. "Get Grandad out of here!"

"Oh no," says Grandad, shaking his head. "I'm not going anywhere without you two. I'm still the grown-up here!"

"Grandad." Rose's voice is firm. "We know what we're doing; you're in our world now. Stay with Win and we'll follow on Vlad." Then, before he can protest, Rose slaps Pickle's side and cries, "Gobet obout obof hobere!"

Pickle spins around and Grandad has no choice but to throw his arms around Win as they lurch through the smoldering door and disappear down the smoke-filled passageway.

Rose and I run toward Vlad.

A cry makes me look up. Now that the flames have stopped, Crowky is standing on the edge of the balcony. He throws himself toward us, wings spread wide, screaming, "YOU WILL NEVER ESCAPE!"

Rose has scrambled onto Vlad's back. "Arthur!" Her hand stretches toward mine and I take a leap and grab it. I'm climbing up Vlad's back when a scratchy hand clamps around my ankle. As Vlad lumbers toward the doorway, Crowky tries to drag me off the dragon's back.

I kick out again and again, and manage to wrench my foot free just as Vlad jumps forward. I keep hold of Rose's hand as we tumble out of the chamber and into the darkness of the passageway. Vlad picks up speed and I pull myself onto his back as flames and smoke and Crowky's cries of rage chase after us.

CHAPTER 42

The dragons race through the tunnels of the Crow's Nest, bumping against the walls and sending bricks and dust crashing down. I try to cling on to Vlad and keep my head low, but it's impossible not to get scratched and bashed about. To add to the chaos the dragons are overexcited and keep breathing out fire, making flames crawl along the ceiling.

Slipping and sliding on Vlad's back, we dash past the cells, Pickle just ahead of us. Then the ground begins to shake.

"What's happening?" shouts Rose.

I look back. At first all I can see is smoke, then two red eyes emerge, glowing like burning coals and moving closer and closer.

"It's Bad Dragon . . . she's chasing us!" The smoke thins and I see Crowky hunched on her back, his face contorted with rage and delight. "Crowky's with her. They're catching up!"

Pickle tumbles down the curving tunnel and we follow on Vlad. Rose bends forward and murmurs in Vlad's ear.

Immediately he picks up speed, taking huge leaps and forcing Pickle to move faster too.

We burst into the round chamber and the dragons keep going, stumbling down the staircase, desperate to get out of this maze of smoke and stone. A fresh wave of fire sweeps past my face. Bad Dragon thunders closer. Then Pickle crashes out into the sea cave, and we follow on Vlad. The two dragons launch themselves off the rocky ledge. Their wings open and they shoot past the *Raven*, heading for the mouth of the cave. Vlad is flying so close to the sea that waves splash against my scorched feet.

This time the dragons don't need to be told; they tilt onto their sides and fly straight out of the cave. I'm hit by blinding light and fresh air. I take huge, deep breaths, trying to soothe my burning lungs. Up ahead Win punches the air and Grandad lifts his face to the sky and smiles. The dragons seem just as happy. They toss their heads about in ecstasy, snapping at the air and stretching out their wings.

But our freedom is short-lived.

A rumbling growl tells me that Bad Dragon is still behind us and when I look back I see that she's gaining on us and fast. Crowky said he could fly again, but he could never fly as fast as Bad Dragon. Her wings are enormous and after being kept in that pit it looks like she's got energy to burn. She soars toward us and Crowky is a huddle of black feathers perched on her back.

"Rose, we've got to go faster!"

She urges Vlad on, and as he rises higher, above the Crow's Nest, I catch a glimpse of the Lost Girls storming the ramparts. I know they've nearly won because the scarecrows aren't a pack anymore. They're on their own, fleeing in ones and twos, and disintegrating into piles of straw as the Lost Girls throw themselves at them.

Then one of the girls spots us and she must say something, because suddenly they're all looking up, pointing and waving. I don't wave back. This isn't over yet.

Vlad shoots straight over their upturned faces, heading back toward land. I look over my shoulder. Bad Dragon is almost within striking distance. "Rose, we can't outrun her. She's too fast!"

"Then we get Grandad to safety." She edges Vlad alongside Pickle and the dragons fly side by side. "Win, take Grandad back to your cave, and make sure no one follows you!"

He glances across at us. "What about you two?"

"We'll follow, but first we're going to sort out Crowky. And, Win, if anything happens . . . take Grandad home."

He salutes and steers Pickle away from us.

"What do you mean?" shouts Grandad, twisting around on Pickle's back. "What could happen?"

"Nothing!" shouts Rose, then she swings Vlad around before Grandad can say another word.

I watch Grandad and Win go. It feels so wrong leaving him just after we've gotten him back, but Rose is right: we have to draw Crowky away. He wants us alive, but he's made it clear that he couldn't care less what happens to Grandad.

Rose guides Vlad back across the Bottomless Ocean, urging him on faster and faster. We fly past the Crow's Nest, the cold air smacking into us, and we keep on going. Bad Dragon follows. Far in the distance, I can just see the frozen peaks of the End.

"Rose, is that where we're going?" I say. "The End? We'll never make it!"

"I know," she mutters, then she jabs her knee into Vlad's side, making him turn sharply. Now we're flying back the way we just came, heading straight toward Bad Dragon and Crowky. Rose glances back at me. Her eyes are blazing and she has cuts on her face and ashes in her hair. "Bad Dragon will never recognize me as her master if I run from her."

"But you're not her master now. Crowky is!"

Rose shakes her head. "Who hatched her? Who trained her? Who taught her how to throw fire? Me!" She leans forward and whispers in Vlad's ear. He responds immediately, rising up so that we're still flying toward Bad Dragon, only now we're coming at them from above. Seconds later, Bad Dragon glides below us.

Rose gets to her feet.

"Rose . . . what are you doing?"

"This!" she cries, then she runs along Vlad's wing and throws herself into the air.

I watch in horror as Rose free-falls through the sky, arms spread wide, before slamming down with a thud on Bad Dragon's back.

"Toburn, toburn!" I yell, digging my knee into Vlad's side. As the dragon turns I keep my eyes glued on Rose. She's getting to her feet and Crowky is approaching her.

I watch as they face each other. Rose is wobbling as she tries to keep her balance. Crowky is strong and sure-footed. He takes a swipe, and she ducks, but then he lunges, grabs her by her shoulders and tosses her to one side like she's a piece of rubbish. Rose rolls along Bad Dragon's back and before I know what I'm doing I'm up on my feet and running along Vlad's wing too.

"Leave my sister alone!" I scream as I jump and plunge through the sky.

CHAPTER 43

At first I don't think I'm going to make it, but at the last moment Bad Dragon's body whips around and I smack onto her back.

The air's punched out of me, but I force myself up onto my knees, then my feet. Rose is lying curled on her side with Crowky standing over her, his fingers spread wide as if he's trying to decide what to do to her. With a yell I charge and Crowky looks up just as I slam into him. He staggers back, then finds his feet and knocks me back like a fly. But I'm not about to give up. He might be stronger than me, but I'm angrier. No one hits a Trout and gets away with it.

I run at him again, only this time I go low and manage to throw him off-balance. He grabs hold of my T-shirt and we tumble across Bad Dragon's back and along her wing. We throw wild punches and kicks. Straw bursts from Crowky and the dragon's hot, rough scales graze my skin. I slip and almost fall, and that's when I look down and see that the *Raven* is following us. Like a shadow, she chases after us, her leathery sails unfurled and a crew of scarecrows scurrying across the deck.

Bad Dragon twists her head and snaps at me and Crowky. We roll in different directions, only I go too far and almost slide down the side of her stomach. I stop myself from falling by grabbing hold of a spike, and I dangle there for a moment, kicking the air, before I find the strength to pull myself up. That's when I see that Crowky has given up on me and is creeping toward Rose. She's whispering in Bad Dragon's ear. She doesn't even know he's behind her.

Crowky lifts his hands above her head.

"NO!" I jump to my feet, run forward, and throw my whole body at Crowky, wrapping my hands around his face. In one smooth movement we flip sideways and tumble off Bad Dragon's neck, falling down toward the Bottomless Ocean.

For a few seconds we're locked together as Crowky tries to pry my fingers off his face and I refuse to let go. Then he stops fighting and opens his wings and starts to fly. He takes me up in the air with him, his whole body trembling with each flap of his wings, the seams on his neck bulging.

"This is the problem with you, Arthur Trout," he hisses. "I need you, but you drag me down." Then his teeth sink into my hand and pain shoots through my body. My fingers start to slip from his face. "I think I'll make do with one Master of Roar!" he says, kicking me in the stomach.

Then my worst nightmare comes true. I'm falling through the air, with nothing to grab hold of, tumbling toward the churning waves.

CHAPTER 44

As I fall, a hollow, cold terror fills me.

I don't scream. I can't. Instead I watch as images flick in and out of my vision. I see Rose kneeling above Bad Dragon's head . . . the black sails of the *Raven* . . . Crowky swooping around me like a bat . . . then Bad Dragon's eyes fix on me, narrow greedily, and her jaws drop open.

I start to clutch at the air, desperately trying to get hold of something. Finally Bad Dragon is going to be fed.

She dives, opening her jaws so wide I can see the fire glowing in her throat. *This is it*, I think as I clutch at nothing. *This is how I die.*

Then I see Rose climb to her feet. I keep my eyes fixed on her and she looks at me. Her face is the last thing I want to see, not Bad Dragon's stained teeth.

Rose raises her fist in the air. "HEAR ME ROAR!" she cries, her voice echoing through the sky. "HEAR ME ROAR!"

Immediately Bad Dragon's jaws snap shut and she ducks her head. Instead of the slash of teeth or the icy rush of the

sea, I feel scales scrape my skin as I slam down on her head. Relief floods through me as Rose grabs my T-shirt, holding on tight, and we start to rise in the sky. I scrabble backward to the safety of Bad Dragon's back. Crowky is directly in front of us, hovering in the air, his wings flapping furiously.

Bad Dragon sighs out a jet of flame and it singes Crowky's wings. Howling with rage and pain, Crowky spins through the air, then smashes into the Bottomless Ocean. His wings fan out, keeping him afloat for a second, but the waves are too ferocious and they crash down on him.

"We can't leave him!" cries Rose.

She's right. Crowky may hate us, and have done terrible things to Grandad, but *we* made him. Seeing him struggling in the water is a chilling sight.

"Dobown!" she tells Bad Dragon, but before we can reach the spot where Crowky is flailing, the *Raven* appears and a rope is slung into the water. As we turn and rise back over the Crow's Nest, Crowky is hooked out of the sea, his body heavy with water, his wings looking battered. Before he's even pulled on deck his head lifts and swings around. I know he's looking for us.

"Time to go home?" says Rose.

I'm so exhausted all I can do is nod.

We fly away from the Crow's Nest, the *Raven*, and Crowky. Already the Lost Girls have raised their flag and it's fluttering over the battlements: it's a skull with a bow perched on its head, a rainbow of color, just like their bracelets. Black smoke drifts about the turrets and the Lost Girls stand silhouetted against the sky. Stella shades her eyes and waves a hand and we wave back. They watch us as we fly away.

The Crow's Nest belongs to them now.

We head inland and Bad Dragon follows the line of the coast, lazily beating her wings and making the Bottomless Ocean surge below her. Vlad appears behind her, then flies in her wake, following like a shadow.

I look across at Roar. The sinkholes have vanished and so has the crack. Before my eyes, leaves burst open on the trees and vines unfurl, sending green spilling over the cliff. Flowers creep out of the gaps in the chalky rock. The Roar Rose and I loved is coming back.

We fly over a long, wide beach. Waves tumble over each other and the dragons' shadows soar over the wet sand. When the cliff reaches its highest point we turn and glide inland. And that's when we see it.

Standing on the edge of the cliff, its horn glittering in the

sun, is a unicorn. Its coat is deepest black and it's covered in spots of silver and pale blue. This unicorn has freckles.

"They've come back," says Rose, her own brown freckled face lit by the sun.

Suddenly she sits up straight, scanning the cliff and the woods. She nudges Bad Dragon back out over the sea, and stares down at the waves. I know who she's looking for: Mitch.

She sees something that makes her gasp. "There!"

Just below the surface of the water is a ribbon of bright blue. It could be a shoal of fish. It could be a reflection of the sky. But just maybe it's the trailing hair of a merwitch.

There is a splash, and the blue is gone.

We circle over the same spot—once, twice—but whatever was there has vanished. We turn and fly across Roar toward Win's cave. We need to take Grandad home.

CHAPTER 45

We land Bad Dragon in a clearing close to Win's cave and Vlad thuds down behind us. Pickle is already there stretched out in the sun.

We half fall off Bad Dragon's back, then watch as the three dragons eye each other warily. After some huffing and puffing, and a little bit of teeth gnashing, they settle down in the long grass, Bad Dragon sitting apart from Vlad and Pickle. She stretches out her long neck and keeps her red eyes firmly fixed on the smaller dragons.

"Shouldn't we make them fly off somewhere?" I say. "If Crowky comes after us, he might see them and find Win's cave."

Rose shakes her head. "We're fine. You saw Crowky's wings. He's not going anywhere."

For now, I think.

Rose goes to each dragon in turn. She rests her cheek against their snouts and whispers in their ears. For a moment she disappears in a cloud of smoke seeping from Bad Dragon's

nostrils. She's saying thank you and goodbye.

I don't risk getting so close. Instead I give them a respectful salute, then we walk into the wood that leads to Win's cave.

We find Grandad propped up by the mouth of the cave, eating an apple and watching Win practice his moves. "This is my very, very best one," says Win as he jumps in the air and does a somersault with no hands.

"Fabulous!" says Grandad, making Win beam with pride, then he looks up and sees us walking toward him. "There you are!" Grandad may be smiling, but he looks terrible. His face is bruised and his hair is singed. Black soot from the dungeon covers his cardigan and even though he's only been gone a few days, he looks skinnier, fragile. Possibly for the first time, Grandad looks like an old man.

"What I fancy right now," he says, pulling us to him, "is to go home and have a nice cup of tea . . . and maybe a bath."

Win looks up in alarm. "You can't go. Not yet. I can do tea. I could probably even sort out a bath, although I usually just jump in the waterfall."

"Tea would be good," I say, looking hopefully at Grandad.

He laughs and nods. "Fair enough. The bath can wait, but a cup of tea and maybe a bit of toast would be just the ticket."

Win jumps to his feet and soon we're sitting around Win's fire, eating bees on toast and drinking Win's milky tea. Afterward Grandad nods off and we drape one of Win's sleeping bags over him. Rose keeps glancing at him, and I know she's thinking that we should get him home, but I can't leave Roar. Not yet.

The day starts to drift toward evening. Birds fly down to the forest, the red ones that go "Pow! Pow!" and fluffy yellow ones that look more like chicks. Some settle in the trees, others hop around on the rock eating our crumbs. Some fuzzies come out of the forest too. They fly right up to our faces. They peer in our eyes and ears. One drops down on Rose's lap and just lies there, staring up at her, saying, "ROSE!" every now and then.

Then we start to talk about the Magic Road, and the

Crow's Nest, and everything that happened today. Rose doesn't mention the flash of blue and neither do I. But we talk about everything else, interrupting each other and going over the best bits again and again until there's nothing left to say.

"So Crowky definitely didn't follow you?" says Win, his eyes shooting toward the forest.

"He couldn't," says Rose. "His wings were burnt and he was half drowned. We left him on the *Raven*. The Lost Girls have the Crow's Nest now."

"But without the Magic Road and the *Raven* they're trapped in the castle." Win looks at me hopefully. "Maybe we could help them build a bridge, or a boat . . ." He wants us to stay. I understand. I want to stay too. "And when Crowky comes back he's going to be mad about the whole 'Lost Girls in his castle' thing. We could probably do with a bit of help."

"Don't worry," I say, looking out over Roar. "We'll be back. Right, Rose?"

She holds up her wrist, where her bracelet of sea glass and shells catches the light from the fire. "Definitely. I've got to give this back to Mitch."

Seeing the bracelet makes me think of something important. "Win, I need you to give me the Relic of Arthur."

His eyes widen and his hand clutches at his chest. "Why?"

"Look, I trust you with it, but, like you said, imagine if Crowky got hold of it? All he'd need to do is crawl through the tunnel and then he'd be in our world, and our world and Crowky would be a seriously bad combination."

"What's the Relic of Arthur?" says Rose.

"This!" Win holds up the fidget spinner on its chain. "It's how I got into your grandad's attic."

"He only got through to Home when he was wearing something that belonged to us," I explain. "It's why I had to get my watch and socks back from that merboy."

"You don't need to come to us," Rose says. "We'll come back to you."

"When?"

Rose and I look at each other. Mum and Dad are picking us up in a couple of days, then we're starting secondary school. "We'll come back as soon as we can," I say.

Reluctantly Win takes off the fidget spinner and places the chain over my head. "Ninja promise?"

I nod. "Ninja promise." Then I say something I know he's not going to like. "I'm sorry, Win, but we need all our other things back too: the rain boot, the putty. It might not just be the Relic of Arthur that lets you through the tunnel."

Win sighs deeply, then gets to his feet. "Come on," he says as he trudges into the forest.

Rose can't quite believe what she sees in the cave. She runs her fingers over the hoof prints and gazes at each object in turn. "I looked for this everywhere," she says, picking up a cuddly toy owl that's missing both eyes. "I thought Mum chucked it out."

We collect everything in the knitted hat and rain boot.

Win insists on putting each object in himself. "Goodbye, chips," he says, dropping the empty bag in the boot. "Goodbye, hair clip. Goodbye, T-shirt." He rests the T-shirt against his cheek for a moment before putting it on top of the other things.

"Well, that's it," he says, looking around the now empty cave.

I shake my head and hold out my hand. "Putty." With a sigh Win pulls the putty out of his pocket. "You don't need it," I say. "I did a ninja promise. We'll be back."

After one last stroke of the tin, he drops it into the boot.

CHAPTER 46

It takes some time walking to the On-Off Waterfall. Grandad is still wheezy, Rose and I are exhausted, and Win is doing everything he can to delay us—ninja moves, stealth walks, bad magic. Plus it's hard to rush when Roar looks so beautiful. Soft sun shines through the trees, and butterflies and fuzzies fly around us. Every now and then we catch a glimpse of the sun setting into the Bottomless Ocean. "Incredible . . . ," Grandad keeps saying. "Just incredible."

When we can hear the crash of water from the On-Off Waterfall, Orion appears. He thunders up to us—desperate to see Rose before she leaves—and then sniffs her hair and face as if he's checking she's OK. Rose clambers onto his back for the last bit of the journey. She tries to get Grandad on too, but after he's stung by Orion's tail he decides it's not worth the risk.

"Sorry, Grandad," Rose says, but she doesn't look sorry when she buries her hands into Orion's mane and rides along with her eyes half closed with happiness.

When we reach the pool Rose slides off Orion's back. The waterfall suddenly crashes down, making Grandad jump and covering us all in a fine spray.

"Will you look at that?" says Grandad, laughing and letting the cool mist fall on his dirty face. He looks at me and Rose and smiles. "You know, this whole place is quite amazing."

After Rose has said goodbye to Orion, Win leads us in a limping line up a path behind the waterfall. Soon the path becomes a series of rocks that jut out like stepping stones. Every now and then water thunders past, forcing us to stand close to the rock face. Grandad is so distracted that I have to keep a close eye on him to make sure he doesn't fall into the pool below.

Eventually we get to the mossy ledge and the four of us squeeze together. Behind the curtain of leaves is the tunnel that will lead us back to the cot and home.

Grandad shakes Win's hand. "It's been a pleasure to meet you, young man. I wonder if I could ask you to do me one last magical favor?"

Win's eyes light up. "Anything!"

"I need a bit of energy, just to see me along this tunnel."

"I know the perfect spell."

Only it turns out Win doesn't know the perfect spell. While he waves his wand in the air and tries out different words—"Basket tail . . . no, *wind* tail, no, *maiden grizzle?*"— Rose and I take one last look over Roar.

I let my eyes run all the way along the river as it twists and turns. I see the Tangled Forest and the dark blue Bottomless Ocean. Then I stare at the End. There is so much of Roar that we didn't get to see. Purple smoke floats around us as Win cries, "Imp grass! No. . . . Imp *glass!*" and fizzing stars start to pop. I know I have to take Grandad home, but I don't want to go. I feel at home here. I *belong* here.

"You know, you're going to be fine at secondary school," Rose says.

"Stop reading my mind."

"Never," she says.

Win must have remembered the right spell because there is a bang and a sudden puff of yellow smoke that twists around Grandad, leaving him with a faint sparkle. "That hit the spot!" he says, then he turns and disappears inside the tunnel.

Now it's Rose's turn. She gives Win a long hug. "Keep looking for Mitch for me," she says. Then after gazing down at Orion, who is still standing by the pool, watching her, she crawls through the curtain of leaves.

Win throws his arms around me. "I've had *the best* adventure, mate."

"Me too." I squeeze him tight. "It's been imaginary."

When he lets go I tuck the boot and hat under my arm and quickly duck under the leaves into the tunnel. I don't look back. I can't.

"Hang on," says Win. "I'll light your way with a little bit of Win-magic." Before I can stop him he sticks his wand into the tunnel and yells, "Sapphire ferret!"

I crawl after Grandad and Rose surrounded by thousands of blue stars. The stars follow me down the tunnel, lighting it up, and only begin to fade when the stone under my fingers disappears and I'm crawling over soft mattress.

I see a bright light and I move toward it until I'm rolling onto the attic floor.

Rose is slumped against Grandad. The old rocking horse glares at me from the corner of the room. "I'm so glad you both decided to play," Grandad says, then he has a puff on his inhaler and leans back in the sun.

I put the rain boot and hat stuffed full of our things on the floor. Then I take the fidget spinner off. I hold it in my hands.

"Do you think it has to be something that belongs to us?" I say.

Rose looks up. "What do you mean?"

"To get into our world? Does someone from Roar need to be holding something that belongs to you or me . . . or could it be anything that comes from here?"

"Like what?" she says.

"Oh . . . nothing." I decide there's no point mentioning that Crowky still has Grandad's "NO PROB-LLAMA!"

T-shirt. I mean, what are the chances of Crowky wearing it if he ever goes into the tunnel? Almost zero, I decide as I clamber to my feet, then I push the thought away.

Rose and Grandad join me.

"Does anyone fancy fish and chips?" Grandad says.

"With mushy peas," says Rose, slipping her arm around Grandad's waist, then the three of us trudge down the attic stairs, a few stray blue stars and wisps of yellow smoke floating along with us.

CHAPTER 47

One week later, Rose and I are walking toward Langton Academy. The sky is gray, my blazer is enormous, and I really wish I hadn't let Mum cut my hair last night.

I feel nervous, but not a-dragon's-about-to-eat-me nervous, so nothing I can't handle.

"I wonder what Win and the Lost Girls are doing," says Rose.

I look up, surprised. We've not talked much about Roar since we got back. Rose has come up with a theory that what happens in Roar must stay in Roar in case the universe gets mucked up. She says it's to do with physics and too complicated for me to understand, but really I think it's because Roar is impossible to put into words, not without sounding weird, and Rose still doesn't like sounding weird.

"Wrestling?" I suggest. "Or maybe they're all at the Crow's Nest having a barbecue."

Up ahead I see Langton's gray walls and the high-security fence that surrounds the school. My stomach squeezes. If the cot was in front of me, I'd dive straight in.

Seeing as Rose is breaking her no-speaking-about-Roar rule, I decide to ask her a question. "Rose, you know when you said that flying was the second best thing that's ever happened to you?"

"Yeah . . . ?" she says suspiciously.

"Well, what's the best thing?"

She rolls her eyes. "Making Roar with you, obviously."

She's right. It is obvious.

We haven't forgotten our promise to Win; we're going back as soon as we can persuade Mum and Dad to drive us over to Grandad's and leave us there for a few days. We've already told them that we need to help Grandad finish the den and half-term isn't far away. Meanwhile, we've decided to get fit. Since we got back, Rose has been swimming every day, and like Win I've been eating lots of apples. I'm building up to the push-ups.

We spent the day after we got back patching up our cuts and bruises. Mum thinks all three of us crashed our bikes when we were out mountain biking. She wasn't quite so convinced when I told her my sneakers got so bashed up I had to throw them away.

"Really, Arthur?" she said, eyes narrowed.

"Actually they got burned off my feet by a dragon."

"Very funny," she said, before agreeing to buy me a new pair.

Grandad also took us to choose our paint for the den

and now it's sitting up in the attic waiting for us. One half of the attic is going to be yellow and the other half will be navy blue. I chose the blue and it's exactly the same color as the Bottomless Ocean. The cot is tucked away under the eaves, next to the paint and Orion, and that's where it's staying.

"Rose!" The shout comes from over the road where three girls—Angel, Nisha, and Briony—are waving like mad. "Walk with us!" Nisha calls.

Rose glances at me. "I'm fine," I say. "I've beaten my nemesis. I think I can handle a few teenagers on my own."

A group of older Langton boys sweep past us, knocking my bag off my shoulder.

"Well . . . you didn't actually *beat* your nemesis," says Rose. "He escaped. In a boat."

"Details, Rose, details."

"Walk home together?"

"All right."

She grins and punches me on the shoulder. "See you later, Arthur."

"Yeah. See you later, Rose."

Just before she crosses the road she pushes up her sleeve and there is Mitch's bracelet. "So I don't forget," she says, then she goes to join her friends, where she's greeted with a flurry of squeals and hugs.

I pull down on my rucksack straps and walk on toward the gates of Langton Academy. I might be short and I definitely can't play football, but that's fine. Because I know who I am.

I'm Arthur Trout, Master of Roar.

Believing is just the beginning.
Get ready to . . .

RETURN TO ROAR

Leaving the island behind us, we walk back across the frozen sea. Rose carries the box as carefully as if it were a baby. The lid of the box is loose, but we've got nothing to keep it down. No tape or string. I tell myself that unless someone opens the box we're perfectly safe, but still the loose lid makes me feel uneasy.

When we arrive at the forest we speed up, desperate to get to the safety of the ship. We follow our footprints, our cold breath billowing out around us. Like dragons, I think, wishing one of the dragons could be here with us now, protecting us, filling this icy world with fire.

Rose comes to a sudden stop and Win and I bump into her. Her hands tighten on the box.

"What is it?" My eyes flick into the snow-heavy trees.

"I thought I heard something," she says, and for a moment we all stand and listen, snow squeaking under our feet, our breathing heavy.

"I heard it too," whispers Win. "It was just a tree moving, right?"

Rose shakes her head. "It sounded more like . . . feathers."

"No," I say. "You're imagining it!"

But just then something in the branches of a tree catches my eye: a flash of black, two glittering eyes, a wide grin. Cold shock punches into my chest.

Rose's voice explodes in the silence of the forest. "RUN!"